THE MUTATIONS

THE MUTATIONS

JORGE COMENSAL

TRANSLATED FROM THE SPANISH

BY CHARLOTTE WHITTLE

FARRAR, STRAUS AND GIROUX

NEW YORK

Farrar, Straus and Giroux
120 Broadway, New York 10271

Library of Congress Control Number: 2019018889
ISBN: 978-0-374-21653-5

Designed by Jonathan D. Lippincott

Our books may be purchased in bulk for promotional, educational,
or business use. Please contact your local bookseller or the Macmillan
Corporate and Premium Sales Department at 1-800-221-7945, extension
5442, or by e-mail at MacmillanSpecialMarkets@macmillan.com.

www.fsgbooks.com
www.twitter.com/fsgbooks • www.facebook.com/fsgbooks

1   3   5   7   9   10   8   6   4   2

PART I

And you have the sinking feeling
that a misprint slipped into the crossword
and made it unsolvable
—Rosario Castellanos

1

Standing in front of the mirror, Ramón opened his mouth like an angry baboon confronting its own reflection. Though he tried to see down his throat, the dim light in the bathroom at La Montejo, his favorite cantina, failed to reach the spot where he felt a pain so searing and exquisite it made a gallstone seem like an insignificant country cousin. He knew as he closed his mouth that the pain would make it impossible to eat the spicy pork sandwich he'd just ordered. He straightened his tie bitterly, turned his back on his reflection, and left the bathroom. A client awaited him at their table, where they were about to celebrate the favorable outcome of an administrative hearing. Ramón summoned the waiter and asked him to pack up the sandwich to go and bring him a chicken lime soup. He felt unpleasant spasms in his tongue as he spoke. He would have to be stingy with his words, and tolerate the dismal soup the waiter brought him instead.

Before they began to eat, the client raised his tequila to

toast their triumph in court. "Your health," Ramón replied, never suspecting that the next morning he would wake with a paralyzed tongue, unable to form the consonants needed to utter those happy words again.

"*Ma mou i uur,*" he said to Carmela, his wife of twenty years. She was alarmed. Instead of giving Ramón a dose of cough syrup like the day before, she made an appointment with the family doctor to whom she usually took their teen-age children, Mateo and Paulina, when they had a bad flu or needed a note to get them excused from school.

"From what your wife tells me," the doctor said, "it seems like we might have a little inflammation of the thyroid. Any tingling in your hands or feet?"

Ramón shook his head.

"All right. Let's have a look, then."

He took a headlight and attached it to his forehead with an elastic strap.

"Now let's open our mouth nice and wide." The doctor was used to treating children, and spoke in a manner Ramón found patronizing. "That's right. Very good."

The baboon reappeared, and the doctor inserted a tongue depressor into its gaping mouth. As soon as the instrument touched Ramón's paralyzed tongue, he felt as if he were being examined with a cattle prod, or perhaps an ice pick. He thought of the techniques used by trial lawyers to interrogate suspects and was sure that under these conditions he would have said anything to end the torture, whether it was true—that he'd always had the hots for his sister-in-law Angélica—or false—that it was he who'd killed Luis Donaldo Colosio, the presidential candidate gunned down in Tijuana. But the doctor was searching for a secret Ramón could not confess.

"We have some unusual swelling here," he concluded after removing the depressor. "Let's do an ultrasound and take a look at what's going on."

He added that it might be a case of sialolithiasis, an infection caused by a salivary stone. Three weeks were wasted as they tried to confirm this diagnosis. Meanwhile, the presumptive salivary stone expanded, causing the tongue to swell at an alarming rate. When he observed this, the doctor referred his patient to Dr. Joaquín Aldama, "a highly experienced oncologist."

Ramón and Carmela were more distressed by the idea of seeing an oncologist than they were prepared to admit. They suffered their anguish in silence. Though they tried to make light of the appointment scheduled for December 4, they decided not to tell their children, who were in the midst of their end-of-semester exams. Mateo was in his last year of high school, and Paulina was in her first. While Mateo attempted, as far as his innate idleness allowed, to pass the four classes he usually failed—math, chemistry, physics, and history—Paulina aspired to crush her only rival, the arrogant and diminutive Jesús Galindo. Focused on achieving their academic goals without forsaking their respective hobbies of masturbation and karaoke, Mateo and Paulina were oblivious to their parents' suffering.

At Ramón's legal firm, Martínez and Associates, the unresolved cases began to stack up. There were certain matters only he could settle, especially those needing to be lubricated with alcohol. Mario Enrique López, the owner of Sagittarius

Real Estate, rarely made any decision without first imbibing at least half a bottle of rum. The firm's public relations depended entirely on the charisma and eloquence of Ramón Martínez, Esquire, but the impairment of his tongue was beginning to undermine those qualities. The sound of his own voice made him feel like a deaf-mute thief had stolen his body; in the mirror he now met with a face much fatter than usual, bitter and frowning, with a mouth stuffed full of cake.

Unable to raise his voice as usual, Ramón took to venting his anger behind the wheel, making his car bellow on his behalf. He pounded the horn to hurry distracted drivers at stoplights, scatter arthritic pedestrians, or simply to blare his frustration at rush-hour traffic. The car's nasal, impotent honk was a cruel reminder that he wasn't driving the powerful German car he'd always coveted, but a four-cylinder Japanese knockoff with fake leather upholstery.

On Friday, December 15, after a painful biopsy in which several millimeters of his tongue were extracted with a thick needle, the most decisive part of the wait was finally over. A team of pathologists in the hospital basement analyzed the cells with a range of antigens and solutions to reveal their nature under the light of a microscope. The report was sent to the oncologist's clinic. There it waited, in a sealed envelope, for the doctor to explain the results to his patient. That was still several hours away.

Husband and wife arrived early for the appointment, and sat down beside an enormous ornamental fish tank. Carmela picked up a magazine and began leafing through it. Ramón fixed his gaze on the aquarium and began to worry about his recent absence from work. He thought he should send his clients Christmas baskets to reward them for their patience and loyalty to the firm. Ramón was known for his strong relationships with his clients, whom he charmed with a well-balanced mix of irreverence and flattery. Besides that, he wasn't hypocritical, opportunistic, or corrupt. He always acted in strict accordance with the law, or at least those laws with which it was convenient to comply. Heaven knew both local and federal regulations were plagued by omissions and inconsistencies that not even the most virtuous jurist could navigate without contention. Given his spotless track record, however, Ramón was sure his reputation wouldn't be damaged by a streak of ill health.

The aquarium distracted him from his woes. A dozen tropical fish swam laps around the tank, which was furnished with rocks and coral. It was a hypnotic dance. How could the oceans contain such an array of patterns and colors? Biologists put it down to natural selection—a slow, accidental process that little by little refashioned all creatures, transforming colossal dinosaurs into defenseless poultry. Every rotisserie chicken was a poignant reminder of the twists and turns of fate.

Carmela interrupted his musings with a friendly nudge.

"Look," she said, showing him the magazine. It was open to a photo of a young couple posing in front of a castle. "Remember?"

Ramón nodded. They had spent their honeymoon in France, and he remembered it well. Carmela turned the page. The couple from the previous photo were now half naked and sunning themselves on a yacht. The caption described them as newlywed Spanish aristocrats. For his part, Ramón considered the aristocracy a regressive abomination.

———

Twenty years earlier, Ramón had met Carmela beside the buffet at a birthday party for his law school friend Luis. He'd noticed her as soon as she arrived, and waited intently, drink in hand, for the right moment to strike up a conversation. When he saw her leave her friends and approach the table, he made his move.

"Have you tried the chorizo *sopes?*" he asked her warmly, convinced that the best way to break the ice was through her stomach.

There were two possibilities: either she had, or had not, tried the chorizo *sopes*. (In those days, vegetarians were so unusual that this likelihood needn't be factored into the equation.) These two possibilities branched off into four potential answers: If she replied that she had indeed tried them and they were delicious, his advances could continue aggressively. If she admitted that she had tried them but made no further comment, he would have to proceed with caution. If she had not tried the *sopes* and indeed did not care to, the mission would have to be aborted. But if she hadn't tried them, and proceeded to take one, he would be close to full triumph. Ramón was convinced he had every possible outcome under control, but he hadn't considered the chance that she might respond analytically.

"Yes. The chorizo is good, but the *sopes* aren't."

"Really?" said Ramón, taken aback.

"They taste like cardboard," she explained.

"Interesting," he said, nursing his wounded pride. "I'm going to have another and see."

"Go ahead," she said, turning and heading over to another corner of the party.

Ramón was left alone with a paper plate loaded with traditional Mexican party snacks. He found a strategic spot to observe Carmela, who was sitting with a couple of friends. Ramón took a bite of the *sope* and savored it carefully without letting her out of his sight. He left his plate on top of a cabinet and went over to where Carmela was sitting.

"Excuse me," he interrupted her, "I just wanted to let you know that you're absolutely right. They're just not the same after they've gone cold. Actually, I brought them myself . . ."

"Oh, I'm so sorry, I didn't realize," Carmela said, struck by the formality of this young man who, instead of showing up at the party with a bottle of vodka and a bag of ice, had taken the trouble to bring a dish of *sopes*.

"No, really, it's fine, I'm glad you told me. You have no idea how good they are when they're fresh, though. I said to Luis—who by the way is my dearest friend—'Fear not, I'll bring you the best *sopes* in Mexico City.'"

"They're really that good?"

"I'd swear it solemnly in front of a notary," he said, "but they have to be nice and fresh."

Carmela, who was also a lawyer and worked at a firm with its own doleful notary, laughed heartily at the seriousness of Ramón's advocacy for his *sopes*. Her uninhibited laughter left him defenseless. He was floored by the perfect Cupid's bow of her lips, her straight, flawless teeth, and her dark, perfectly outlined almond eyes. A flame melted his composure. He fell silent, averted his eyes, and pretended to lose himself in the swirling pattern on the carpet. And now what do I say? he wondered.

"Where did you get them?" Carmela asked.

"It's a secret," he replied, coming to his senses.

"Oh, really?"

"I don't even know your name."

"Carmela."

From that moment on, Ramón was unstoppable. He was witty and charming. He told amusing stories and asked flattering questions. He managed to rein in his usual loquaciousness. Carmela told him about her plan to become a civil attorney. She was brilliant. He was so thrilled by their conversation that he didn't dare go back to the buffet for fear of losing her. Despite being hungry and sober, he left the party ecstatic.

The next Monday, Carmela received a bouquet of roses at her office, along with a calling card that said in elegant, printed letters, RAMÓN MARTÍNEZ, ESQ. ATTORNEY. Underneath were some handwritten words, plagiarized from an Armando Manzanero song: *When roses look redder and more beautiful, it's because I'm thinking of you.* She didn't recognize the quote, but it didn't bother her, though her sentimental education owed more to fashionable Spanish bands like Mecano and Presuntos Implicados—a far cry from a crooner of romantic ballads from Yucatán. When Ramón called the next day to ask if the roses had arrived, Carmela's voice betrayed her blush as she thanked him. Then he invited her to dinner on Friday evening. She accepted.

Ramón arrived to collect her at the appointed time.

When Carmela's mother, Antonia, answered the door, she discovered not the elegant, polite young man she'd been expecting, but a mestizo. Carmela's mother belonged to the most ambitious subgroup of the Mexican middle class, and since Ramón's dark complexion interfered with her racist social aspirations, she didn't invite him in. "Just a moment," said his future mother-in-law, before practically closing the door in his face. In his mind, he was still waiting on the steps for Carmela to emerge when a feeble elderly couple crept grimly into the waiting room.

The couple greeted Dr. Aldama's receptionist like an old friend, then sat down opposite Carmela and Ramón. When he saw how slowly and tentatively the old man took his seat, Ramón surmised that he must have prostate cancer. Poor bastard, he sympathized, he must have to piss sitting down. I should start going to the urologist, I probably have an enlarged prostate, too. It's natural. But that thing where the doctor sticks his finger up your . . . I hope I don't get a hard-on.

How far he was at that moment, as he waited to see the oncologist, from the young Ramón who got turned on whenever he saw Carmela come out of her office in a tailored suit. After two months of chaste encounters in cafés and restaurants, it was Carmela who'd suggested that they go somewhere else. Ramón took her to a motel in Colonia Roma. They finished undressing clumsily between clean sheets in a dark room, and just as he kissed her with all the thirst of his twenty-eight years, he heard the receptionist's piercing voice call his name, twenty years later, announcing that his turn had finally come to see Dr. Aldama.

2

Teresa de la Vega, a psychoanalyst, saw her patients in an office built onto the old house she had inherited from her parents. When she was forty-four, her mammary glands, fourteen lymph nodes, nipples, and areolas had all been surgically removed. She possessed the deep and penetrating gaze of someone who had known the fruits of beauty and intelligence, but not of happiness. Her only marriage, fifteen years earlier, had ended after eighteen months, due to the paranoia of her husband, a psychiatrist and prescription drug addict, and Teresa's inopportune affair with another psychiatrist who was more talented and attractive than the first. They had not had children.

After her divorce, Teresa went on meeting her lover, in secret, since he was also married. One day, as he massaged her breasts vigorously, she felt his hand recoil, startled, as if it had touched an insect. Her lover still went on thrusting, but kept his hands away from her chest. She faked an orgasm so it would be over quickly, then went into the bathroom to examine herself in front of the mirror. As soon as she detected the small, hard lump, she knew that history was repeating itself; her mother and sister had both had breast cancer. She was so afraid of the disease that rather than keeping watch for it with frequent checkups and mammograms, she had always shied away from an intimate relationship with her breasts. She'd never imagined that a man with the hands of a Vietnamese baker would be the one to bring her to face a misfortune whose origin stretched back beyond her memories of her mother's illness—far beyond, to the ancient tribes of Israel.

Three thousand years before Teresa, on the banks of the River Jordan, lived the ancestor—perhaps a shepherdess or a weaver, a warrior or a whore—in whom the founder mutation occurred. Perhaps this was during the period of Second Kings, under the rule of Amaziah or Jeroboam.

Perhaps.

In any event, it came to pass one morning, at some unremarkable moment, as she approached or departed the well, as she prayed, as she cooked or wove, that one of her germinal cells abruptly began to divide. Day after day, all day long, it had transcribed its usual set of instructions, its Books of Law, its genetic Torah, but today, in slipped a misprint, like an error in the Book of Exodus, had the scribe forgotten to include the essential "not" in chapter 20, verse 13, leaving the sacred commandment to instruct us, "Thou shalt kill."

The chances that the error would persist were slim; eukaryotic cells can contrive to correct their genes, and if these happen to be broken beyond repair, they're capable of committing suicide by apoptosis—a premeditated and altruistic death. But our biblical misprint took place in a passage dedicated precisely to preventing the wrong cells from proliferating and establishing anarchist communes in the bosom of the imperial body. In 1990, the gene in question entered the language of science, and was named, with neither tact nor imagination, Breast Cancer 1. This initial mutation consisted of the omission of two simple DNA letters, G and A, guanine and adenine, usually found near the beginning of the lengthy gene sequence in question. The mistaken text endured thanks to its host's abundant, scattered progeny, and at last reached the body of a young psychoanalyst in Mexico City.

When Nebuchadnezzar the Great conquered the kingdom of Judah, the mutant's children were already abundant, and many were imprisoned and driven into exile in Babylon. So began the erroneous gene's diaspora to Iran, Egypt, Iberia, Holland, Bulgaria; if you search among the Sephardic Jews of the Aegean Sea or the Ashkenazis of New York, the misprint can be found in at least one in every hundred passersby who observe Shabbat.

But Teresa de la Vega wasn't Jewish. Her parents had been steadfast Catholics, devotees of the Virgin of Guadalupe, staunch nationalists, and even vaguely anti-Semitic. She never imagined that the first Jews of Castile could be found in her family tree—immigrants during the Roman period, modest city dwellers untouched by internecine conflicts, vassals of the Goths and caliphs alike. They worked at the fringes of society. They knew how to read and write. They intermarried. They abounded in wealth, traditions, and mutations. The envy of others ripened, and the fifteenth century saw it bear fruit. They were found guilty of killing Christ, of prospering, of devouring the children of Toledo, of bewitching the virgins of Seville, of burning crucifixes, of having large noses, of sodomy, of not eating bacon, and of usurious collusion with the devil.

In the year 5252 of the Hebrew calendar, the king and queen of Castile and Aragon decided to expel the infidels. They gave them four months to leave or renounce Judaism. Perhaps among the wretched converts was an elderly woman, Lorenza, a resident of Soria, mother of eleven, and widow of a man named Manuel. Just before turning seventy, she began to feel burning in the tips of her drooping breasts. Weeks passed. The fire spread to her armpits. Lorenza sought the help of Herminia Tavares, a converted Christian and sorceress, for a cure for the pain and swelling. In exchange for three silver coins per dose, Herminia prepared her a tincture to heal her unbalanced humors.

When she began to treat herself with that salve of garlic and nightshade, the cancer had already spread to her brain. She was plagued with headaches and hallucinations. In the straw of her bed, she searched for a knife to decapitate herself. Then an angel of the Lord appeared before her, to torment her for betraying her tribe. She cried out her renunciation of the false messiah: "Lord, have mercy upon me, wash away my sins."

Her neighbors went before the court of the Inquisition. An infidel possessed by the devil, a sinful old hag; God the Father had punished her with a vicious affliction of the breast. Her children took her to an orchard far from the city and muzzled her cries. Herminia prepared an opium brew to ease her suffering. She died in early winter. They buried her beneath a lime blossom tree in the countryside and recited the Mourner's Kaddish in whispers.

From then on, Lorenza's family was marked by suspicion. People spat at them in the street as they passed by. Fernando, the youngest son, was the first to flee. He arrived in Cádiz in February. He had never been to the coast before. The ocean reminded him of a scorched wheat field.

In early March, he set sail on one of the humblest boats in the West Indies fleet. It was bound for New Spain, where, word was in the taverns, gold and silver sprang like turnips from dry earth. He spent forty days at sea, suffering from fevers and constant hunger. He passed the time playing cards and watching the largest galleons in the fleet sail unflaggingly ahead, their sails billowing to the west, leaving a trail of tumultuous foam in their wake. Thus, his fantasy, a ship loaded with ambition, sailed toward the forgetting of his blood. But on board the galleon was his semen, the essence of memory and mutation.

Fernando disembarked at the port of Veracruz. He fled the pestilent coast on a cart bound for the capital. After three toilsome years, he took a common-law wife, the illegitimate mestiza daughter of a man from Asturias and an Indian woman. Half a world was erased in that meeting of genes from Judea, Asturias, and Texcoco—but thirteen generations later, Teresa's body remembered it.

———

She didn't bother with the unnecessary transaction of seeing her usual doctor. She looked up the number of the oncologist who'd treated her mother and called to make an appointment. The result of the mammogram was clear: three adenocarcinomas in the mammary ducts, which had never known the reprieve provided by breastfeeding.

After surgery and ten rounds of radiation, Teresa went back to seeing her patients. During her treatment, she had met several women struggling not to succumb to depression in the face of their illness. She offered them psychological support at no cost, and thus began to specialize in psychotherapy for women with cancer. The news spread from hospital to hospital that Teresa could help women grieving the loss of their feminine attributes. Some men also began seeking her services. The first, a survivor of cancer of the esophagus, needed help quitting smoking. The second had tried to kill himself when he was diagnosed with cancer of the penis. The third had lost his twin brother to an osteosarcoma. In this way, her range of patients broadened until it included cases as diverse as childhood leukemia and bouts of hypochondria triggered by the TV series *House*. "Why me?" asked most of her patients, as they tried to comprehend the scale of their misfortune, but Teresa, who years earlier had consigned that narcissistic question to the garbage, tried to lead them down a different path, into the basement of unfulfilled desires that fed their fear of oblivion.

3

Carmela wondered how to break the news to the children, forgetting that Mateo was already eighteen, and Paulina fifteen. By the beginning of the new millennium, adolescence had become a self-absorbed extension of childhood. Yet armies of spoiled brats—among them Mateo and Paulina—had still, by varying means, managed to trade their innocence for angst and their cuteness for acne.

"Your dad has something a little more serious than we thought . . . He has a tumor in his tongue, and unfortunately the only way to remove it is an operation that . . ."

There was an excruciating silence.

"What?" said Paulina.

"They have to remove the whole tongue," Carmela went on, in tears. "We've seen three different doctors, and they all think there's no way around it. The tumor's in a dangerous place, and they have to make sure they get it all out. They said if they could, they'd shrink it with radiation . . . but there isn't time for that, right?"

Ramón had been in his own world, his eyes fixed on the carpet. He nodded.

"No way," said Mateo. "Rafa had his gallbladder removed through a couple of little holes. Like, no big deal. How come they can't do something like that?"

"That's what we asked the doctors, but . . ."

"So how are you going to talk?" Paulina asked her father. Ramón looked at her with the weariness of someone already and continually facing that very mystery.

"There are some speech therapies that might help," said Carmela.

"How?" asked Paulina.

Carmela couldn't begin to know how to answer.

"Can't they give him a fake one? Like, made of plastic?" Mateo asked. "That would be awesome."

Ramón was exasperated by the way his son spoke—loud and moronic, just like the trashy music he was always listening to. "You'll go deaf," he'd often warned him, but he hadn't foreseen that long before that happened, he himself would be mute. Ramón tried not to think about it, since the woeful scenes he pictured made him regret having agreed to the surgery. It seemed like a simple choice, life or death, but in his situation, as a self-employed lawyer with no health insurance or retirement plan, who made a living from his way with words and from manipulating the law in court, it was anything but. To stifle his worries, he turned on the TV at night and cranked the volume all the way up. "You'll go deaf," his son might reasonably have admonished, and Ramón would have ignored him like a teenager convinced of his immortality and eternal youth.

———

Carmela didn't hesitate to tell Elodia, the family's maid, that Ramón had cancer of the tongue, and would soon go into the hospital for a serious operation. Elodia knew immediately that this was a test sent by God to restore Señor Martínez's faith.

When Ramón came downstairs for breakfast, Elodia went to greet him and blessed him ceremoniously, slowly drawing the sign of the cross in front of his face.

Ramón was a staunch atheist, but he tolerated Elodia's piety, since the pair enjoyed a long-standing complicity. Whenever Carmela discovered an offense committed by one of them—a towel hung incorrectly, a stained tablecloth, a rumpled rug—each took the blame for the other, so as to bask in the glory of domestic martyrdom.

Elodia was six years younger than Carmela, who had hired her soon after the couple moved into their first house. When Elodia got pregnant with the gardener's child, Carmela urged her to have an abortion.

"I'm the one who sinned, señora. It isn't the baby's fault," Elodia answered, outraged by the suggestion that she murder her child.

"It's not that anyone's to blame, but you're too young to be a mother."

"The Virgin Mary had little Jesus when she was fifteen. Imagine if Joseph had said, 'That child isn't mine, now run along and get rid of it at the clinic.' It's not right, if you think about it."

Six months pregnant, Elodia married Salvador, the gardener, in the groom's hometown of Atlacomulco. He turned out to be a disreputable, philandering, drunken, and belligerent husband. Elodia endured ten years of marital torment, until the day Salvador "got carried away" and knocked her unconscious.

When Ramón saw her black-and-blue face and her toothless mouth, he was possessed by a bitter thirst for revenge, and promised Elodia that he would make sure that criminal never set foot in her house again. He went to see his contacts at the district attorney's office, slipped them an envelope full of cash, and asked them to go forth and mete out justice. "Tear him a new asshole," he specified. Neither Elodia nor the neighborhood gardens ever heard from Salvador again.

One morning, several years later, Ramón found Elodia crying in the kitchen. Someone had called from her village to say that her mother, who had kidney disease, could no longer get out of bed.

"They told me her legs are swollen and her blood needs cleaning, but it costs a fortune."

Ramón had just upgraded his car and bought plane tickets for a family vacation to California.

"Bring her to Mexico City," he said, choking down a certain amount of selfishness. "I'll help you pay for it."

That was how Ramón became benefactor to an elderly diabetic who survived eleven months longer at a cost of two dialysis sessions a week and a dozen brand-name medications.

He also footed the bill for her body to be transported back to the tiny cemetery in her hometown.

From then on, Elodia's gratitude toward her employer transformed into open veneration. She placed a photograph of Ramón on her homemade shrine, just to the left of God. Yet despite his holiness, Ramón never tired of blasphemy, proclaiming religion to be a scam, the Catholic Church a cadre of child molesters, and atheism the only path to Mexico's salvation.

Once, when Ramón's gold watch went missing, Elodia found herself accused of theft. Before confronting her, Ramón gave his daughter the task of spying on the suspect's every move. He bribed Paulina with a doll's house in exchange for any valuable information. After a week in this role, the only odd behavior Paulina could report was that every day, Elodia spritzed the family's beds with a clear liquid she kept in a spray bottle. When interrogated, she confessed that it was holy water.

"And what if it's dirty?" Carmela asked.

"How could it be? The sacristan fills the font with bottled water."

In the end, the watch turned up in Ramón's desk drawer, where he had stowed it a few weeks earlier before going out to lunch at a cheap restaurant in Tepito.

When Ramón got sick, Elodia went to the city center to buy an image of San Peregrino, the patron saint of cancer patients, and stuck it to the Martínezes' fridge door with a souvenir magnet from Acapulco. Beneath the picture of San Peregrino was a prayer Elodia recited every time she took something out of the fridge:

OH! SAN PEREGRINO:
YOU who are called the Wonder-Worker,
Because of the numerous miracles God has bestowed
upon you,
YOU, who bore in your own flesh the cancerous dis-
ease and who had recourse to the source of all Grace
when the power of man could do no more.
YOU were favored with the vision of Jesus coming
down from His Cross to heal your affliction.
Ask of GOD and OUR LADY the cure of the sick
whom we entrust to you.
(Insert name of patient)
Amen!

(One Our Father, Hail Mary, and Gloria)

In exchange for Ramón's miraculous recovery, Elodia was willing to give up avocados, her favorite food. Perhaps if she'd had any true vices, she might've been in a better position to bargain with God the Father. As the date of the surgery approached, Elodia increased her sacrificial offerings: in the end, she gave up tamales, soft cheese, and *chile de árbol*. She also begged her mother's spirit to put in a good word on her boss's behalf, imploring her to remind God how kind Ramón had been to her before she died.

Magical thinking took hold in the Martínez household. Despite Ramón's anticlericalism and Carmela's lukewarm religious feelings, their children went to a Catholic school, where they were exposed to mass on a regular basis, took the required catechism classes, and attended talks about the perils of premarital sex. Paulina began visiting the school chapel every day. Mateo had a feeling that his daily masturbation habit might interfere with his father's recovery, so he resolved to stop watching Internet porn and touching himself. Carmela began calling the bank compulsively to check her balance, as if some miracle might multiply their savings overnight, thereby solving the problem of how to pay for the upcoming surgery plus two weeks of postoperative care in the Metropolitan Hospital. It was so blatantly reckless of them not to have health insurance that she was ashamed to admit it in front of her friends and family. Her sister Angélica spared no words in reprimanding her when Carmela turned to her for a loan.

"We can lend you fifty thousand pesos, but that's all."

They needed twenty times that much, equivalent to Ramón's annual income, from which they had to subtract tuition and the monthly payments on the car, the truck, and the three computers that Ramón had bought in January for his children and secretary. Ramón had invested all his savings in remodeling his offices and was too proud to request a loan from anyone outside the family. His only hope was his younger brother, Ernesto, a self-made millionaire with a Styrofoam packaging factory.

After failed incursions into importing third-rate Spanish wines, and manufacturing fruit jams for diabetics, and low-fat tamales, Ernesto threw in his lot with Styrofoam, the pure-white miracle of the petrochemical industry that had revolutionized fast-food packaging and classroom dioramas. He began to manufacture disposable packaging just as takeout became widespread, and demand for his products skyrocketed overnight. In a little less than a decade, Ernesto's business, Styromex, Inc., had come to dominate the Styrofoam market all over the central plateau of Mexico.

From the beginning, Ernesto had asked Ramón to take on all the legal aspects of his business: contracts, lawsuits, severance packages. Unlike his older brother, Ernesto was a ruthless boss, a dishonest competitor, and a chronic tax dodger. After winning countless crooked cases in his brother's favor, Ramón had decided to stop working with him.

"Your problems don't leave me enough time for my own clients. I'm finding you another lawyer."

"Family first," Ernesto answered.

"Right, but you don't listen to me. You're always cheating your suppliers, firing people, forging receipts . . . I can't work like this."

"How much do you want?"

The argument ended in a string of insults peppered with truths—that Ernesto was an alcoholic and Ramón suffered erectile dysfunction—and lies—that Ernesto was illegitimate, and Ramón a homosexual. When Ernesto claimed that Ramón was just rotten with envy and called him a fucking hypocrite, Ramón hung up on him. Over a year passed, and they hadn't spoken since. Carmela was determined that if they weren't going to ask for a loan, they should at least let him know about the surgery, and wait and see if he offered to help. Ramón was convinced that he wouldn't make any such offer and only allowed Carmela to call Ernesto so he could prove himself right.

"Tell me how I can help," Ernesto said, genuinely distraught by the news of his older brother's cancer.

Carmela explained the situation and Ernesto agreed to lend them the money, on one condition.

"To avoid any misunderstandings," he told his sister-in-law, "we'll draw up an IOU for the amount of the loan and use your house as collateral. It could be mortgaged if necessary, right?"

Ramón was outraged by this miserly proposal. That little shit didn't even know the meaning of work until after he finished college. And who paid his way until then? Who bailed him out when he got arrested for drunk driving in Mom's car? I did. And now he asks you to sign an IOU, like I'm a fucking stranger. He should loan me the money and take me at my word, as a sign of trust and to show a modicum of gratitude. I'm not letting you sign shit. I'll sign it myself, and if I die, he can go fuck himself.

With the help of a handwritten note, and using a different vocabulary, Ramón let Carmela know his decision.

"Don't you think he'll back out?"

He doesn't have the balls, thought Ramón.

4

Eduardo went to therapy every Saturday at eleven sharp, armed with an aluminum bottle of ozonated water and a clean sheet to cover the promiscuous couch where he had to recline during the session. He was Teresa's favorite patient, not for his extravagant phobias, but because he was young, and because he had sought her help not to come to terms with the idea of having cancer, but to free himself from its hold on him. He'd had leukemia between the ages of nine and twelve and had been cured by multiple rounds of chemotherapy and a stem cell transplant. Despite his successful treatment, though, he had never recovered any sense of himself as a healthy young man. Now, at nearly twenty, he was convinced the disorder must still be lurking in at least one of his two hundred and six bones. Along with his acute fear of microbes and contagious illness, this prevented him from leading a normal life. He had braved high school in latex gloves and a surgical mask and been taunted and made the target of endless pranks. On one occasion, a gang of troublemakers had taken a bag of dog feces to school and emptied it into Eduardo's backpack during one of his frequent trips to the infirmary. When Eduardo returned to the classroom and opened his pack, he keeled over in fright. He awoke besieged by the smell of shit and the sound of his classmates' merriment and was paralyzed by a fear so corrosive that his teacher had to carry him back to the infirmary. He never went to school again. In just two years, he completed his high school diploma online, and passed the university entrance exam in Hispanic literature with the highest possible score.

Eduardo's specific aim in going to therapy was to learn to endure the ordeal of his college classes. He was studying at the National Autonomous University, whose campus, in his opinion, looked more like a low-budget prison than a UNESCO World Heritage Site. His plan was to graduate as soon as possible and get a job as a copywriter, editor, or translator—anything that would allow him to work from home, without having to be exposed to the contagious hordes of his peers.

He arrived late to therapy only once, when his mother's car broke down and he had to walk for over an hour to Teresa's house. He entered her office panting and red in the face, his clothing soaked in sweat. Teresa knew he hadn't taken a bus or a taxi, because he was incapable of boarding any form of public transport without having a panic attack.

The chemotherapy that had cured his leukemia had also temporarily destroyed his immune system, and the twilight of little Eduardo's childhood consisted of an endless succession of protective antiseptic measures. Teresa believed that beneath the manifest cause of his germaphobia lay a repressed attachment to his illness, an unresolved and unspeakable grief for his cancer. This symptom, which she had observed in several young patients, was analogous to Stockholm syndrome, in which a hostage develops an unhealthy affection for his captor.

"Why do we have to carry something foreign inside us that isn't us?" Eduardo had asked her once, when discussing his intestinal flora. Teresa, astonished by the psychoanalytic resonances of the question, quickly scribbled it down in her notebook. Eduardo also had an aversion to all that was white. "That color turns my stomach," he would sometimes say, a remark Teresa found curious, since white generally symbolizes all that is pure, and good, and clean. In Eduardo's case, the essence of the Lacanian Other was the danger that lay in wait, the invasion of the leukemia that threatened to poison his blood with whiteness—with abnormal cells that were, precisely, white. The sheet Eduardo used to cover Teresa's couch was sometimes blue and sometimes green, but never white. Sheets, gloves, surgical masks . . . his identity depended on those barriers that shielded him from the contagious, pathogenic, life-threatening Other.

Eduardo's mother had nurtured her son's neuroses. The fear of losing Eduardo, her only child, the result of a brief affair, had made her a stickler for diet and cleanliness, and indulgent in all other matters. By catering to his every taste and whim, she had allowed Eduardo to become accustomed to getting his way. When Eduardo asked Santa Claus for an industrial air purifier made in Japan, his mother spent her entire Christmas bonus acquiring it. Eduardo was a voracious reader who detested bookstores and libraries and sent his mother out to buy him books, which had to be new, since he'd reject any that didn't come wrapped in plastic. When Eduardo decided to start keeping kosher, his mother was forced to adopt all kinds of dietary restrictions, though neither she nor anyone she knew was a practicing Jew. Her son proclaimed the wisdom of kashruth's prohibition of pork and shellfish, genuine vectors of bacterial sin.

And though he never raised the subject during their sessions, Eduardo's celibacy was clearly tormenting him more and more. His frustration was obvious to Teresa. But how was he ever going to sleep with a girl if he wouldn't even let his own mother give him a hug? When would he ever be able to penetrate a mouth or a vulva if he felt such revulsion toward bodily fluids? The challenge was great, but so was the reward, Teresa thought. If anything could save him from his phobias, it was the persuasive power of Eros.

Yet Eduardo despised his college classmates, and usually referred to them as "Neanderthals." He was already about to finish his first semester, and still hadn't made a single friend.

"I think they've infected me," he said with deathly seriousness on the first Saturday of December.

"With what?" Teresa asked him, keeping her expression neutral.

"Some kind of fungus. Candida or aspergillus. I don't know which, but I have symptoms of fungemia."

"Such as?"

"Chronic fatigue, memory loss, anxiety, hot flashes. I don't have any respiratory or GI symptoms, though. I probably have fungi in my bloodstream. I've started taking fluconazole, but it's not working. It's my mother's fault, she made my coffee too strong one morning, and since it's a diuretic, I had to go to the bathroom at school. You should've seen how much yeast and mildew is growing in there—it's horrific. I'd already told her to use only two spoons of coffee on days when I have class, so I don't have to go. 'I forgot,' she said. But whatever, I had to use the bathroom and breathe in all the filth in there. Staph bacteria, spores . . . The humidity disperses the microbes. It's horrendous. It's not just my hypochondria, I swear. I've been feeling terrible. And the problem is, it's really hard to detect fungi in a blood culture. And you know how much I love getting my blood work done . . . This is a disaster."

"Why didn't you just go home?" Teresa knew that in the past, as soon as Eduardo had needed to pee, he'd called his mother to pick him up and take him home, which wasn't far.

"I couldn't."

"Why not?"

"I'd agreed to help a classmate study linguistics at one, and I didn't have her number to cancel. But then I started feeling too ill to stay, anyway. I told her I had a family emergency and then I left."

"And did you arrange to meet some other day?"

"No. I felt like throwing up, and I couldn't stop thinking about all the urine and microbes I'd stepped in. They put cardboard under the urinals to absorb the splashes, but it's so disgusting. Cardboard is the perfect fungal breeding ground. I couldn't stop thinking about all the filth on my shoes. I could feel the flagella tickling my legs, creeping up my leg hair, getting up into my—"

"You didn't realize the bathrooms would be so dirty?"

"I knew they would, but I had no choice. My class ran over and didn't finish until one-fifteen, and I'd agreed to meet this girl in the library at one."

"When did you agree to meet?"

"Monday. She asked to see my notes because she'd missed a class, and I told her someone else had already asked me. Obviously, that wasn't true, but I wasn't about to lend them to her . . . so I told her if she wanted, on Wednesday, I could explain what happened in class."

"And do you think she got hold of the notes?"

"Yesterday we had a literature class together, and at the end she asked if everything had worked out with my emergency. I said yes, thanks, everything was fine, and asked if she wanted to do the linguistics stuff, but someone else had already lent her the notes. That's all. And it's just as well, because that's when I started feeling worse, right when finals are coming up. It's a disaster. I can't focus on anything. I keep thinking about all the fungi in my bloodstream, and whether they're crossing the blood-brain barrier . . . I can't handle it."

"I remember studying with a friend when I was in college, and it helped a lot. We took turns explaining the topics and then quizzed each other. It worked out really well."

"Emilia isn't my friend, she just happened to need some notes, and then I had to go use the bathroom just because I tried to be nice to her, and now I have a fungal infection that could turn into a generalized septicemia."

Teresa felt a special kind of sympathy for Eduardo. In her own therapy sessions, she had talked about him and the maternal instinct he aroused in her. She would have liked to ask him, "Why don't you invite her out for coffee?" but the suggestion would have put him on the defensive. Eduardo's body had let him down too early in life, and he couldn't get over that betrayal. In one of his first sessions, he told her that he took so many hygienic precautions because his body was incapable of taking care of itself, and he had to do so on its behalf. "Aren't you your body?" Teresa had asked him, and Eduardo had responded, "The body is mine, but it isn't me."

Denied the blessing of a healthy childhood, Eduardo set out on a mission to safeguard, through a strict regime of nutrition and hygiene, the life of which the symbolic Other had threatened to deprive him. He had accepted that task as his destiny, the meaning of his existence. It was unthinkable to part with such a treasure—even when its care turned out to be a nightmare. Leukemia had determined the course of his life, had promised him its cure would be paradise, but then, when he was finally given the all-clear, Eduardo found himself abandoned to the mercy of an uninspiring adolescence, an overprotective mother, and a world indifferent to his health. His disillusioned mind found refuge in his phobia, in the unrelenting struggle against germs and the ghost of leukemia, foes that allowed him to keep believing in the happiness that lay ahead. In this way, the order signified in the Lacanian metaphor of the "Name of the Father" could be preserved.

———

Teresa wrote down the name Emilia in her notebook. The night before, she had smoked some marijuana, and her memory was still hazy, slippery. She grew the plants herself on her rooftop, in a locked room illuminated by high-pressure

33

sodium lights and ventilated by an extractor fan. She had started smoking pot to counteract the nausea, loss of appetite, and headaches caused by chemotherapy. The experience had made her a fervent promoter of marijuana, as much for recreational as for medicinal purposes.

Whenever her patients needed help coping with the side effects of radiation and chemotherapy, Teresa would offer them, in a whisper, a session with Mary-Jane, the miraculous herb that soothes pain, heightens the senses, stimulates the appetite, and even inhibits the cancerous maggots that gnaw away at our health . . . Eduardo, she thought, would benefit from giving it a try. Most of the buds she harvested in her greenhouse were intended for use by her patients in cancer treatment. She kept a small amount aside for her own spiritual benefit.

5

The night before the surgery, Paulina went online to ease her uncertainty. She typed "total glossectomy" into the search field, read the paltry Wikipedia article, then proceeded to view the images Google produced. Ghastly. She was forced to interrupt the consumption of her second Twinkie of the evening. Ever since she was small, Paulina had curbed her anxiety by bingeing on sweets, but the sight of those pictures killed her appetite. She lasted less than a minute in front of that grisly collage of mutilated mouths, stitched-up wounds, and mishmashes of bloody oral tissue. She closed the tab quickly and took refuge in scrolling through Facebook, where life went on uneventfully amid retouched photos, inspirational quotes, cartoon memes, and music videos. Once she'd regained her composure, she bit into the Twinkie, opened another window, and swiftly typed in the word "cancer." She clicked on Wikipedia again and began to reread the article, as if preparing for an exam on the subject. "Cancer is the name of a group of related diseases involving abnormal *cell* division." The hyperlinks were displayed in blue. "It can begin in a localized manner and spread to other surrounding *tissue*. If the patient does not receive adequate treatment, cancer often results in *death*." There were three hyperlinks to choose from. She decided to start with "*death*." "Death is the cessation of the *homeostatic* process that sustains a living organism and is therefore the end of *life*." If death was a hyperlink, where did it lead? Paulina had trouble believing in the Beyond, but it was comforting to believe in ghosts, since that would mean her father could never completely vanish, unlike his tongue, which would the very next day. She went back and typed "tongue cancer," her fingers flying like lightning across the keyboard. She had already skimmed all the most popular entries, and this time clicked on "Epidermoid Carcinomas," unaware that these had nothing to do with her father's case. Still, she read in terror, "50% of such growths are fatal." A dreadful word, which, when typed into Google, produced a page about the eighties stalker movie *Fatal Attraction*. A reminder of the Internet's vast indifference to Paulina's hunger and fear.

Only one Twinkie was left in the box. She decided to use it as an excuse to go see Mateo, who was probably still up and would be just as nervous as she was. She took the Twinkie and went out into the hallway, bending down to see if Mateo's light was still on. When she saw through the crack under the door that it was, she approached and knocked. The only discernible sound came from the TV news in her parents' bedroom. She knocked again.

"Mateo," she called.

Paulina pictured him sitting in front of his laptop, surfing the Internet with his headphones on. The scene was accurate, though incomplete, since she failed to include his unfastened pants, his erect penis, his hand moving back and forth, and the eager stepsisters in the swimming pool. Mateo preferred to watch lesbian erotica, since male porn actors diminished his genital self-esteem.

Mateo felt vaguely guilty when he masturbated. Lodged in the depths of that feeling was a slightly absurd but effective image invented by a priest during a sex education talk: "The body of a young Catholic is the Lord's dwelling and a temple to Christ. Touching ourselves with impure intent is like going to a friend's house and bouncing up and down on their bed with muddy shoes. It might be lots of fun, but their bed isn't for bouncing, but for resting, and for celebrating, at the appropriate time, the supreme reward of marriage, which is procreation." But Marisa Johnson, Mateo's favorite porn actress, had an irresistible, angelic moan that matched the two impeccable wings tattooed across her back. Watching her, he enjoyed earth-shattering orgasms that soaked right through the tissues where he spilled his unfruitful seed.

Halfway through a video of Marisa frolicking with her nominal stepsister, Mateo heard the knock on his door, and mumbled a frustrated, "Fuck!" He hurried to close the porn site, pulled up his pants, hid the unsullied Kleenex, shouted, "Coming!," wiped his moist hand on his sweater, stood up, adjusted his penis to hide his erection, walked across the room, and opened the door to his sister.

"Do you want a Twinkie?"

"What?"

"I brought some Twinkies up to my room. Do you want one?"

"Seriously, Pau? I was doing my homework."

"Whatever. Come on, I bet you were chatting."

If Mateo didn't take the last Twinkie in the box, the temptation would be too great for her to resist.

"No, I ate a bunch at dinner . . . thanks," said Mateo with forced politeness, trying to disguise his annoyance at the interruption.

"You could eat it later."

"No, really, I'm good. Thanks. You should go to bed."

"I'm scared, Mateo . . ."

Paulina started to cry. Mateo, ashamed of wanting to go back to Marisa, gave her a hug, taking care not to let his pants brush up against her.

"Don't cry, Pau. You should get some sleep."

Paulina felt like showing him the photos of dissected mouths and amputated tongues she'd found online, to make him realize the full extent of the tragedy awaiting them the next day. She cried tears of anger and terror. Mateo patted her impotently on the back with the affection of a robot. She would have been more consoled by an autistic cat.

After a moment, Mateo broke their embrace, insisted that Paulina go to bed, said good night, and shut himself back in his room. Paulina was left alone in the hallway. She looked toward her parents' bedroom door but didn't approach it. They had too much to worry about; they didn't need her to bother them.

She went back to her room and lay down on the bed.

From the posters tacked to her wall, the cutest boy bands of the moment gazed down at her with smiling indifference. She felt a curious mixture of childish fear and womanly desire. She wanted to hug her father and have sex with Justin Bieber. Her adolescence was a strawberry milkshake of instinct and loneliness. With its golden sheen and sweet, creamy filling, the last Twinkie called to her from inside its transparent package. Eat me, it said, and she obeyed.

After a long period of insomnia in solidarity with her husband, Carmela succumbed and was now snoring like a Viking passed out on grog. At her side, Ramón lay sleepless, imagining a tongueless life, the pity of his family, the confusion of his clients, the impatience of his fellow lawyers and judges. He was about to embark on an eternal game of charades, but with movie titles replaced by legal arguments.

Night slid viscously on. The tumor throbbed in his mouth like a tiny, misplaced heart. Ramón disguised his fear as impatience to get into the operating room, then leave again, maimed but at least having settled the score with his cancer. He counted up all the cancer victims he'd known until then. He'd never paused before to consider just how many there were, which he put down to the excesses of modern life.

At around 3:00 a.m., he finally nodded off. Tell them not to operate, he murmured in his sleep. As he was wheeled into the operating room on a gurney, panic seized him. It was no longer a dream. He was about to be mutilated. A wave of cortisol surged through his body, preparing him to defend himself or to flee. The nurses stationed the gurney next to the operating table and lifted him onto it in a single motion. He was surrounded by doctors and nurses in surgical gowns, caps, and masks. He recognized Dr. Aldama and the surgeon as they greeted him. He could tell they felt cheerful and festive and eager to start carving him up.

A minute of confused preparations went by. A distant voice told him to take a deep breath. He was awake and completely lucid. He was afraid that the anesthetic wouldn't take effect, that he would wake too soon and feel the scalpel, his flesh split open, the spurting blood, the doctors' laughter, the suddenly bare, white bone.

"Relax, Ramón," a voice was saying.

"*I iu aie*," he corrected them. "It's Mr. Martínez," he tried to say, with his tongue, for the very last time.

"Give him some midazolam," said another voice, an echo.

The curtain of night fell over his eyes. Again, the waiting was over.

6

In her sessions with her own analyst and supervisor, Teresa
returned time and again to the question of transference and
countertransference with Eduardo. According to Teresa's interpretation, her patient was transferring the psychological
role of his mother onto his therapist. By caring for him so
obsessively during his illness, his mother, a single parent, had
revealed that the object of her desire wasn't her sickly son,
but rather the hidden, threatening Father beyond, of whom
everyone spoke, though they rarely uttered his name. Cancer
had taken on the unconscious role of the Father. That terrible
identity remained repressed deep in the recesses of Eduardo's
psyche. The object of his mother's desire was the Other in
him; she wanted, unwittingly, for her son to have cancer. It
was an unspeakable horror. That was why his unconscious
worked so hard to repress it. And that symbolic father's phal-
lus, its external symptom, was the cleanliness, the hygiene
Eduardo's mother worshipped. Now, when she attempted to
break her own rules and come close to him without a surgical

mask, to treat him like a normal son, Eduardo sensed the oedipal threat of incest. Betrayal. Letting go of those phallic sanitary measures meant nothing less than killing leukemia, the Father, once and for all.

This psychoanalytic interpretation led Teresa to conclude that her maternal feelings toward Eduardo, which she had often explored with her analyst, were a product of counter-transference, and should therefore be put to use for his psychological cure. Teresa wanted Eduardo to overcome his identification of cancer with the Father, so he could insert a figure into that role that would be conducive to his leading a healthy emotional life, as much on a familial as on a sexual level.

"The problem," said Teresa, leaning back on the couch, "is that I don't see how I can convince the patient that my desire—I mean, I'm talking about the transference, his mother's desire—isn't for him to be sick and have to obey a set of paranoid rules to avoid contagion or a recurrence. I can tell him that, but not on the unconscious level. At least, not right now."

Teresa paused, waiting for her analyst to reply.

"Beyond the countertransference, do you think there's something preventing you?"

"It's not that I'm afraid of wanting to channel my feelings into him because I don't have any children of my own. I've already worked on that. I've talked about it for hours, and I can deal with it. What makes me feel like I'm at a dead end with this patient is that I'm clearly part of the system that keeps him tied to leukemia. He knows I work with cancer patients and run support groups, and that I've written about my own experience with breast cancer. How am I, a psycho-analyst specializing in cancer patients, supposed to convince him that he doesn't have cancer? That's one issue. And the other is, how am I supposed to get him to understand all this when the fact is that I find it fulfilling to see him, I'm fond of him, our sessions cheer me up, and on top of that, his mother is paying me every week? How am I supposed to convince him that I don't want him to stay sick?"

"When it's time to end his analysis, you'll set that part of the process in motion."

"But when?" Teresa protested. "In another ten years, when he's done with college, whereas right now he has the chance to meet people his own age with similar interests? The university is a hive of social activity, and instead of taking advantage of it, he's dealing with an emotional roller coaster—disgust and libido, fear and curiosity. He needs a more immediate solution."

"Well, you may think the solution is to pause his analysis now, and send him to CBT or group therapy, though I guess anything in a group would be impossible for him, but anyway, a cognitive behavioral therapy that would ideally allow him to enjoy life as soon as possible. But I see a projected desire in this rush for him to enjoy things. You're the one who's in a hurry for something to happen. You've never said he shows any interest in going to parties, going out with his buddies, or anything like that. I think your feelings about this are similar to his mother's. You need to be careful, the countertransference could sabotage all your progress with him."

"But what progress? I understand that my concern is maternal and whatever you like, and of course I'm not going to ruin the transference by showing him that. But what worries me is that my strong association with cancer on a symbolic level, as a survivor and a specialized therapist, won't let him get past the idea that what his mother wants is for him to be sick. Just think, when he leaves my office on Saturdays, he sometimes runs into my twelve o'clock patient, a woman in chemo who's lost her hair and walks with a cane. How's he going to overcome cancer like that? As long as he keeps seeing me, he'll still be immersed in it."

"Do *you* still want to be immersed in it?"

"Yes, I do. But him? I'd like to refer him to someone else, but if I do that, he'll have to explain everything again—the leukemia, the transplant—he'll have to relive it all, and that's not what I want for him. It would be a major setback."

There was a pause, during which Teresa imagined the consequences of referring Eduardo to a different analyst, perhaps a young man with whom he could establish a paternal bond. She didn't open her mouth. She knew where her analyst was headed: she wanted Teresa to face the possibility that the unconscious structure she attributed to Eduardo was in fact her own, and that she herself was convinced that everyone else wanted her to keep living with cancer.

"I think my patients want to identify with me as a survivor, and that's the most valuable thing I can offer them."

"A survivor?"

"I know," said Teresa, frustrated that she hadn't seen her analyst's next move coming. "That word. But it's important not to lose sight of the fact that, even if it doesn't define our identities, cancer changed the direction of our lives. It's a constant presence in my life, and I honestly think I've come to terms with that, but Eduardo's case is very different. I mean, I don't think my interpretation of his case is a transference of mine. He's dealing with his phobias, his OCD, his anxiety, the threat of the Real, the grip of leukemia on his ego. It would be great if he could experience something new, maybe with marijuana, and have his mind opened by something that came from outside. I can't offer him that. I'm not going to break the transference and mess everything up, but maybe if someone at the university . . . I don't know. It would be really positive for him."

Teresa paused when she noticed that her analyst had adopted her usual closing gesture. Neither broke the silence. Teresa wasn't keen on variable-length sessions, but her analyst favored the practice, and had ended their talk with expert skill, preventing Teresa from continuing to speculate about Eduardo's case rather than delving into her own conflicted relationship with cancer, the Other that had never ceased to make its unseen claims on her.

After a moment of increasing tension, the analyst stood and wished Teresa goodbye with a friendly smile.

7

Ramón woke up in a tangle of tubes and cables. His consciousness attended to his senses one by one, beginning with his hearing—a strange gurgling in his throat, a machine's high-pitched, intermittent beeping; then his sense of touch—the pressure of the bandages strapping his head to his neck brace; and his sight—the pale light, some gray curtains, his hands crumpled on the bed like dead birds. There were no smells, since the air entered his body not through his nostrils, but through a tracheotomy connected to a breathing tube. Nor were there any flavors, since his taste receptors were gone.

While his brain was gradually rousing itself, his heart pumped a mixture of his own blood and other people's, from bags donated by an airline pilot and a hyperrealist painter. His lungs filtered adulterated air from an oxygen tank, his liver burned its reserves to make up for the fast, his kidneys were busy breaking down the anesthetic, and his pancreas was taking a siesta.

Ramón tried to blink and opened his eyes two hours later. Carmela was by his side.

"How are you feeling?" she asked in a whisper.

What time is it? thought Ramón.

"The surgeon said there weren't any complications, and they didn't have to go in as far as the larynx. And the good news is, you'll be breathing normally in a few months. We're very relieved. Mateo and Pau are out there with Ernesto and Alicia. They send you their love, and they'll be back to visit tomorrow. Elodia was here all day, too, but I sent her home."

Ramón paid close attention to the form, but not to the content of Carmela's words. He was mesmerized by her rapidly moving lips, her expansive vowels, the plosives and occlusions, the sweet harmony of the way they combined. As her teeth moved incessantly up and down, Ramón caught a glimpse of her moist tongue, fluttering and tireless, changing places at every moment to release a succession of different sounds.

He felt a faint pang of nostalgia. Where might his tongue be now? In a Ziploc bag? In a freezer? In a furnace? He had given written permission for samples to be extracted and analyzed in the laboratories of the National Cancer Institute. Apparently, his tumor was unheard-of, and would help researchers to establish clinical precedents. At least it would be of use for something. Beyond that, according to the General Health Law in Matters of the Sanitary Disposal of Human Organs, Tissue, and Corpses, his tongue would have to be cremated, but they wouldn't return it to him in an urn, as if from a funeral home. Where were his tongue's ashes going to end up? Two weeks earlier, it would have seemed like an idle

47

question, but now he regretted not having insisted that its remains be returned to him, however meager they turned out to be. By the time he was well enough to express his wishes in writing, he was sure it would be too late.

Carmela settled in next to him on a recliner and told him to sleep well. He did not. Doctors and nurses kept coming and going, checking his chart, his blood pressure, his catheter, his feeding tube, and his breathing valve. But they didn't interact with him. Instead, they woke him up and prodded and poked him, with neither permission nor apology. They gave him mechanical instructions—"Lift your arm," "Breathe out," "Breathe in," "Open your mouth." They issued warnings—"This might hurt a bit," "Just a little prick," "It'll sting." They asked questions—"How are you feeling this morning?" "Is the catheter bothering you?" "Have we had a bowel movement yet?"—but relied upon Carmela, or one of Ramón's other and more clinical representatives—the thermometer, the urinary bag, or the stainless-steel kidney basin where he spat the saliva that pooled in his mouth—to provide the answers.

———

This same stainless-steel kidney basin featured in a misdemeanor on the afternoon of December 31, when Ramón and Mateo were left in the room alone. Carmela and Paulina had gone out to get sandwiches and soda for their New Year's Eve dinner. While Mateo played video games on his laptop with his headphones on, Ramón dozed off watching a fifties melodrama on TV. When he awoke from his siesta, the movie was over and had been replaced by *Laura en América*, a Peruvian tabloid talk show where guests tried to resolve their family strife in public. Mateo was still stretched out on the couch with his back to his father's bed, shooting his virtual rifle to the rhythm of the heavy metal blaring into his ears. A short woman appeared on the screen.

"He swore to me he'd quit going to the club with his sister, but there he was, drunk, with his arms around her, feeling her up! He's a scumbag, Señorita Laura!"

"Are you telling me your husband cheated on you with his own sister?" the show's host asked in outrage, like the chorus of a Sophoclean tragedy.

"That's right, Señorita Laura."

"Incest!" screeched the host, as the betrayed wife began smacking her sister-in-law and rival.

Ramón was outraged that such degrading spectacles appeared on TV, dulling the mind and inciting morbid curiosity and barbaric behavior. He looked for the remote control to change the channel, but it had been left on the trolley, out of his reach. He needed his son's help, but Mateo was absorbed in his laptop, deaf to any outside noise, and blind to his father's wild gesticulations.

"Bring out the husband!" cried Señorita Laura. When the individual appeared onstage, his wife and his sister-lover pounced on him. Two apathetic security guards intervened to stop them. As soon as the culprit took his seat, the presenter said:

"Not even wild animals do what you get up to, understand? Not even wild beasts in Africa!"

The crowd applauded.

Imagining the cries and insults he would have hurled at

his son didn't make Ramón feel any better. He began to hammer on the bedrail with the basin, inside which a considerable amount of bloody saliva was swishing around, in the vain hope that the clanging would attract his son's attention. Ramón could have summoned a nurse at the mere push of a button, but it seemed absurd to have to do so when his eighteen-year-old son, still a dim-witted mama's boy, was sitting only a few feet away.

"And whose fault is all this? Who raised this pair of perverts? Bring out the mother!"

Under the influence of the talk show's Peruvian rage, Ramón gave in to the urge to toss the stainless-steel basin onto the floor, aiming at the side of the couch to give Mateo a fright. The basin looked like an obese boomerang as it spun through the air, spraying flecks of bloody sputum in all directions. It struck not the floor but Mateo's head, right on the crown, splattering most of its slimy contents onto his open laptop. Mateo sprang up from his seat and turned to his father in fright.

Ramón was genuinely surprised that his arm, in complete contempt of his conscious intentions, had managed to launch the flying basin on such a trajectory. After all, he was right-handed, and he'd had to use his left arm, since the other was immobilized by an intravenous tube. Forgive me, he said silently, sincerely. I didn't mean to, I assure you.

"What kind of a mother lets her teenage children see each other naked?" Señorita Laura demanded to know.

"What the hell?" asked Mateo, more concerned for his bloodied laptop than his convalescent father.

Since he had no way of correcting the misunderstanding, Ramón decided to use it to his advantage and pretend he was afflicted by a stabbing pain in the stomach. Mateo called the nurses' station and asked them to come over because his father was feeling unwell. Señorita Laura and the paid shills in the audience were still shouting their heads off on TV, but for the moment, Ramón decided not to take any further action.

A nurse arrived. She made sure that the feeding tube was in place, then asked for some help from a doctor, who had the good sense to turn off the TV as the incestuous sister hurled a torrent of curses at her cowardly brother.

"Did he throw up?" the doctor asked when he saw the floor spattered with bloody sputum.

"No," said Mateo. "We dropped the spit bowl."

"They'll be here to clean up in a minute," the nurse said kindly.

The doctor palpated the patient's abdomen and came to the conclusion that the pain might have been caused by a minor intestinal spasm. Meanwhile, Mateo shut himself in the bathroom with his laptop and set about wiping it meticulously with toilet paper.

When they were left alone, Mateo apologized to his father for not being more considerate. Ramón, also embarrassed by the incident, forgave him with a smile and excused himself, thinking that, under the circumstances, it wasn't such a bad thing for his act of aggression to go unpunished.

His bout of anger awakened the hunger that had lain dormant during the previous weeks. Ramón's abdominal fat reserves were almost spent, and the protein shakes delivered through his feeding tube were lower in calories than the pork and beans, fried steaks, and *pozoles* that had taken center stage in his usual feasts. Never again would he taste a succulent rotisserie chicken, the complex spices of *mole* sauce, the delicate sweetness of a flan. The loss was great, and irreparable. It was impossible to evoke those flavors; not even their memory would give him solace. The objects of his nostalgia were without qualities, deep and sorrowful chasms in his mind.

Carmela and Paulina returned laden with cartons of takeout, complaining about the lines at the shopping center and the traffic clogging the streets.

"How have you been?" asked Carmela.

"Great," Mateo replied. "We were watching TV."

"Oh, really?" Carmela said suspiciously.

It was also to Ramón's advantage to hide the afternoon's embarrassing episode. He seconded his son's version of events with a serious look.

"Great. Well, we brought some potato salad and cod sandwiches. Let's see if they're any good."

Cod: another delicacy lost to him.

At midnight, Ramón toasted the New Year with a sip of cold water.

8

No matter how sweet, gentle, or gleeful they may have been at birth, oncologists always end up in the grip of melancholy. No other specialist, not even the forensic pathologist, maintains such an intimate relationship with misfortune. The soul of the oncologist retreats so as not to wither. When a terminal patient begs for a morsel of hope, the doctor cannot feed him lies. Duty demands not kindness, but professionalism.

What kind of a calling is oncology? What kind of satisfaction or reward does this specialty entail? What paths lead to this grim career as a spokesperson of misfortune, a dispenser of dire cures and deadly prescriptions? When studying the oncologist's face, it must be remembered that inside lies a motive, a cause, an unconscious trauma, a masochistic heroism, a macabre curiosity; perhaps a desire to emulate his father, to kill or to please him, or just to land a residency in a fancy private hospital. The oncologist's office is a psychological crime scene; behind the diplomas adorning its walls lurk motives that flee the light.

This melancholy physician's heart is as cold as his hands are sterile. The warmth of his patients may fail to stir him, but sometimes an exceptional tumor, a galloping cancer, a lone tiger, awakens his hunter's instinct.

Aldama picked up his phone and called Luis Ramírez, a pathologist at the National Cancer Institute. Two weeks earlier he had asked him, as a personal favor, to take a look at the samples from a sarcoma he'd just removed. Aldama wasn't keen on Ramírez's vulgar extroversion but had turned to him because he was a master at identifying enigmatic tissue and understanding what he referred to as "these fucking cellular idiosyncrasies."

"Did you do a biopsy on Godzilla or what?" asked Ramírez.

"I thought it seemed remarkable right away. I'm very interested to know what you make of it."

"Well, when I first saw the samples, I thought those dipshits had gotten the plates mixed up, so I told them to set up some more, and I couldn't believe my eyes. 'I'll be damned,' I said to myself. 'A pediatric alveolar sarcoma.'"

"But didn't you see the patient's age?" Aldama interjected.

"Damn right I did! 'Holy shit,' I said. 'Not even a manchild like Chabelo could get something like this.'"

"Everyone here was convinced it was a round-cell sarcoma."

"Look, send those little smart-asses from Harvard back to draw blood, that's all they're good for. This is a textbook alveolar rhabdomyosarcoma. I mean, it's like the motherfucker's two years old!"

"But Luis, he's fifty, and there's no family history, and

no mutagens, either. He's a lawyer from Mexico City. I can't explain it . . ."

"Well, me neither. But if we figure it out you can bet they'll give us a Lasker or a Nobel Prize."

"Well, I don't know about that."

"Why not?" Ramírez replied with mock indignation. "When was the last time you laid eyes on something like this? An adult cell that acts like it's in kindergarten! Do you have any idea what that means? We could be looking at the fountain of eternal youth, my friend."

"I have a hard time believing in that kind of thing."

"But you have to admit that it's pretty weird. Is your patient a homo?"

"He doesn't have AIDS, if that's what you mean."

"Maybe not," said Ramírez, "but it looks like he's been sucking some radioactive Superman dick!"

Ramírez's guffaws masked Aldama's awkward silence. He found it disconcerting that such an eminent pathologist could be so crass.

"I'd be interested to know," Aldama continued when the pathologist had stopped laughing at his own joke, "if you think it's appropriate to do a genetic profile to catalog the mutations involved."

"Damn straight. Those cells have got to be given a grilling. They have PAX7 and FOX1 fusions, shitloads of KRAS, NRAS, and FGFR4 translocations, and a whole bunch of other fucking tongue-twisters. I can tell you now, if there's a glitch in the PAX3 gene—the PAX7, whatever—but in the PAX3, at least in childhood cases, that's when the shit really hits the fan."

"I'm afraid the clinic makes it hard for me to stay up to date on oncogenetics," said Aldama. "If you could give me a hand with this and help me chase up the relevant studies, I'd be very grateful."

"If you give me the green light," said Ramírez, "I'll talk to Juan Delgado. He's a geneticist at the university and he's really good at this stuff. I'll tell him, Juan, this sarcoma we have here's a tough motherfucker. We've got to cultivate this thing and study the shit out of it. It's going to have a fuckload of abnormal oncogenes. We could be looking at a cover story in *Cancer*, my friend."

"Do you really think it's that significant?" Aldama asked, incredulous at the pathologist's enthusiasm.

"They divide like crazy, but they're disciplined little fuckers—they adapt and stimulate blood vessels without asphyxiating or blocking each other. It's like a stampede. They're crazy-ass bitches, but really disciplined Asian ones. And what's nuts is how they raise so much hell without crashing into each other. Are you following me?"

For the first time in his tedious career of diagnoses and routine treatments, Joaquín Aldama found himself faced with a mystery: How had such an aggressive childhood tumor appeared in the tongue of an adult male? It was as much of an aberration as finding mariachi rhythms in a Bach composition. What strange mutations were behind it? What risk factors had enabled it? He would have to design an aggressive adjuvant chemotherapy plan.

Aldama fantasized about seeing his name in print in prestigious magazines, being invited to deliver keynotes and seminars in Boston, London, and Paris. He could already taste the fame of having elucidated the causes of a sarcoma even rarer than the one that dispatched Hugo Chávez, the malignant founding cell of the populist tumor choking Venezuela. Aldama's classist convictions were based on a dubious physiological analogy: if there were no hierarchies within the body and all cells enjoyed the same privileges, humans wouldn't be intelligent mammals but sea sponges. That was why unruly cells and mutinous flesh had to be removed, cast out from the organism's social fabric. How to do so in such a difficult case? The tumor had been resected, along with the surrounding tissue, but the cells could easily still be lurking somewhere in the impenetrable barrios of the lymphatic system. If you were a metastatic sarcoma, where would you hide? The lymph nodes would be the obvious place, but apparently, no such luck. It might have decamped to the trachea, the eye sockets, or the commodious thyroid gland. But why the tongue, of all places? When the maxillofacial surgeon had removed it from the oral cavity and placed it on a steel tray, oozing an orange mixture of blood and saliva, Aldama had gazed in bafflement as if at a mollusk, an enormous slug, completely alien to human anatomy. The eye, the hand, the penis, and even the pancreas bear the mark of humanity, but the tongue is an eccentric, versatile organ; the tongue is an artist, a priest of flavor: gluttonous, vociferating, loquacious.

During the patient's fetal stage, a rhabdomyoblast had formed, but never matured. For almost half a century it lay dormant, inert in his tongue. What took it so long to flex its proletarian muscles? How did it manage this? And how many times did it divide before becoming a tumor cell? To find out, Aldama would have to brush up on oncogenetics, and collaborate for the first time with a team of biomedical scientists. Ramírez had convinced him they were going to make a highly unusual and valuable discovery, worthy of presentation before the international scientific community.

Until that work began, though, Aldama would have to make sure that the patient lived long enough to be subjected to exhaustive DNA testing. As soon as he'd recovered from the glossectomy, Aldama planned to begin an aggressive adjuvant chemotherapy regime. He would approach Ramón's treatment with the kind of dedication he had shown only in the case of Lorena Galván, a young woman of searing beauty who had appeared in his office twenty years earlier. Her dermatologist, a former classmate, had referred her to Aldama so he could examine a mole that had sprouted on her left ankle, whose outline bore more resemblance by the day to the shape of the state of Jalisco. Around that amorphous mark, the voluptuous continent of Lorena's physique unfurled, where cells conspired in their trillions to paint a hyperrealist portrait of Parvati, the most sensual goddess of all mythologies. Her face was nocturnal and feline, her body a cocktail of amphetamines, and her voice a bewitching flame.

———

Aldama usually examined his patients with cold, firm hands, but they trembled as they approached those legs tanned by the tropical sun. If it hadn't been for his loose white coat, his trousers would have betrayed a shameful bulge. After a lingering ascent up her legs, he detected something serious: swollen ganglion cysts in the inguinal fold. Aldama had to double his efforts to conceal his ardor and his suspicions: stage IV melanoma type 1b, with an extremely bleak prognosis.

As he sat behind his desk and took the patient's medical history, Aldama peppered her with needless questions, posed with the sole purpose of keeping her in his office. With a warm, paternal demeanor, a far cry from his usual bedside manner, he ended the appointment with a prolonged caress of her shoulder and baseless words of reassurance.

On her next visit, Lorena was accompanied by her fiancé, a dashing and pompous rich kid who jilted her two months later, claiming that he loved her too much to see her suffer. Lorena was devastated by the breakup. From that moment on, as her decline hastened, Aldama's care became increasingly personalized. He went as far as making house calls to inject her with medications he could just as easily have prescribed as pills.

His passion overrode his beliefs and principles. He went from being frank to furtive, from honesty to deceit, from distant examination to gratuitous fondling, from hatred of tattoos to rapt contemplation of the rose that flowered across Lorena's back, the swallow that spread its wings at her waist, always half concealed by her lace-edged panties. Aldama longed to sip the rose's nectar, capture the swallow, perch his bird in depravity's nest. He was even aroused by his patient's whimpers of pain. Overwhelmed by guilt and self-reproach, he considered referring her to a chaste colleague, preferably a blind, female oncologist who wouldn't fall victim to the same perversions as him.

The only antidote to his depraved fantasies was his passion for the works of Bach. No other composer had the power to distract him from Lorena. At home, he withdrew to his study and dosed himself with at least an hour of fugues, cantatas, and counterpoints. He gazed at his records as they spun on the turntable, hypnotized by the spiral orbit of the needle falling to the silent center of the musical galaxy.

Despite his early conversion to atheism, Joaquín Aldama was possessed by spiritual demons. At his Catholic school the Marist Brothers had taught him that the flesh is weak, an enemy of the soul. It had to be fought somehow, with perseverance and privations, with drugs and the scalpel. Wasn't his whole career a battle waged against the ravages of the flesh? He believed it was. Aldama felt an absence of something sacred; he yearned for it. He thirsted after ritual and transcendence, sacrifice and communion; music granted him solace and serenity.

And what was the most powerful remedy for lust? *The Art of Fugue*, played on the harpsichord. Its old-fashioned timbre had a geometric air that swept him into a realm far away from himself, where form stripped down to incorporeal perfection. Side B of the third disc, "Contrapunctus XIV." Aldama was entranced by the three subjects of this fugue. As the piece approached its 170th bar, a fleeting figure in the highest voice ravished him. His shudder could be likened only to orgasm, as intense as it was brief. The composer had left this counterpoint unfinished on his death. In bar 239, the music founders, the air is stilled, a bird flies into a transparent wall, again and again. That pause between music and sound, that ceaseless moment, was Bach's masterpiece. Aldama had often heard the funereal song of an electrocardiogram connected to a dead chest, but death had never sounded this way. There it was.

———

One night, as he savored a Ravel concerto and a single-malt scotch, he received a call from Lorena's father. Despite her narcotic-induced coma, Lorena was agitated and showing signs of pain. Aldama rushed to her house. A jolt of adrenaline cleared the fog from his intoxicated conscience.

He found her in torment amid tangled sheets. He inspected her already purple fingernails and still-fleshy lips, administered a final dose of morphine, and left the room. He caressed each letter of her name with nostalgia as he inscribed it on the death certificate.

Since that encounter, the taste of vinegar had never left his mouth. The years went by, bringing children, records and concerts, patients and disciples, lovers and grandchildren. He resigned himself to growing old, until the challenge of Ramón's case shook him awake.

"How's the duck?" his wife asked him during an anniversary dinner at a high-end restaurant.

Aldama was preoccupied, considering the possible consequences of including doxorubicin or cisplatin in Ramón's chemotherapy. He wanted to add methotrexate, too, but he wasn't sure how it would interact with the other drugs.

"What?" he said.

"How's the duck?"

"Very good," he said, without conviction. He had just read a recent study about the application of high doses of interferon in children and teenagers with rhabdomyosarcoma, but he wasn't familiar with that medication, and he was afraid it might be premature to use it at the adjuvant stage. "And your steak?"

"Delicious," she said enthusiastically. "As soft as butter."

They went on dining in silence.

9

After an expensive two-week stay in the hospital, Ramón went home to continue his convalescence. Elodia was in charge of his care. Carmela, who hadn't practiced law in years, became interim director of Martínez and Associates, where she, two young paralegals, and a secretary trained back in the era of shorthand took on the task of resolving the few cases Ramón hadn't passed on to other colleagues. These were disputes that presented no particular challenge: claims against defaulting tenants, the drafting of purchase agreements, protections from excessive sanctions.

While Carmela updated herself on legal matters, Elodia took intensive nursing classes from a neighbor, a caregiver for elderly people with dementia. She learned to administer injections to a papaya, take blood pressure, and give abdominal massages for constipation. Her most important mission was to enforce the diet prescribed by Ramón's nutritionist. For breakfast, she had to concoct an elaborate smoothie: two egg whites, a cup of milk, half a banana, three-fourths of an apple, four ounces of cooked oats, and two ounces of mango. She arranged the ingredients on the kitchen table, measured out the quantities with alchemical zeal, checked the proportions against the recipe while saying them aloud, then poured them one by one into the blender.

"Señora," she said to Carmela, "can I add some nopal? It's good for the veins."

"Don't improvise. Just do exactly as the recipe says."

"And where am I going to get mangoes?"

"Aren't there any at the market?"

"They don't bring them till April, and that's if it rains."

"The supermarket always has them. Put them down on my list."

The main injunction was for Ramón to gain weight before beginning his chemotherapy. "Shall I bring you another smoothie?" Elodia would ask him compulsively. "Have you finished your yogurt?"

It was also vital to shield him from infection. Elodia doubled down on her efforts to keep the house clean. She scoured the pots and pans furiously, laundered the towels twice over, brutalized the floors with bleach and the carpets with the vacuum cleaner. Ramón took refuge in the bathrooms, which reeked of chlorine, to escape the electric racket sucking up the dead skin from the rugs, the dirt carried in from the street on people's shoes, and the negligible sprinkling of dust continually shed by the plaster walls.

Just as Elodia's workload tripled, her wages were cut. The Martínezes became increasingly indebted to her, and she accepted their partial payment every Friday without complaint. On the contrary, she worked far more contentedly now that Ramón spent his days recuperating at home, at the mercy of her constant chatter.

"Now that you can eat more," she began to say as she vigorously dusted the bookshelves in the study, "I'll make you some mashed *chilaquiles*. You just soak the chips in the salsa, and they soften up all by themselves. You won't believe how good they are." It hadn't occurred to Elodia that Ramón had lost his sense of taste as a result of the glossectomy. "And you know what? They say that chili has healing powers. An aunt of mine had the same thing as you, but in her uterus. They started the injections and it put her right off her food. Then someone told her to put some chili powder on her belly near the tumor, to sweat it out. I'm not kidding. In three months, she was like new. One time I put some chili and garlic on a wart on my elbow. A miracle cure."

Elodia's monologues lulled him to sleep like soft background music. Ramón took long siestas that led to nights of tossing and turning, his insomnia compounded by his oral discomfort and financial woes. To distract himself, he would go down to the study to see what the satellite dish was picking up at that hour: ancient reruns, soft porn, evangelical sermons, and infomercials, nearly all dubbed into Spanish.

What he most enjoyed from among those dismal TV offerings was an infomercial for a case of Japanese Takemitsu knives. It was a multicultural tour de force, featuring a Chinese man dressed up as a samurai and a peroxide blonde whose apron looked like something you'd buy in a sex shop. To demonstrate the knives' power and versatility, the Chinese man sliced through, among other things, a tennis ball, a multivolume encyclopedia, and a frozen turkey.

"That's incredible, John Li," the woman exclaimed, with a smile so stiff she looked like a ventriloquist. "I never dreamed that a knife could do that! But . . . you know what? Whenever I try to slice a pineapple, the knife gets jammed or slips. Once, I almost chopped my finger off! Whatever can I do, John? Do you think these Japanese high-tech Takemitsu knives could help me?"

Next came Ramón's favorite part: the Chinese samurai asked the blonde to take a pineapple and toss it to him like an American football.

"Are you serious, John?"

The Chinese man responded by brandishing the chef's knife like a baseball bat. The blonde tossed the pineapple daintily and John Li sliced it lengthwise in midair. Then the camera zoomed in on one of the perfect halves as it fell to the floor. Ramón was thrilled by this feat and thought it more than worthy of the fake applause on the infomercial.

Had he called in the next five minutes, in addition to a set of fifteen professional-grade knives they would have thrown in an ergonomic potato slicer and a Japanese cookbook. Despite his utter helplessness in the kitchen and his hatred of Japanese food, he wanted to purchase the Takemitsu knives so he could use them in tasks as absurd as those performed in the infomercial. He pictured himself sauntering through the house with the roast beef knife, carving things up for his own amusement. He would have butchered at least half of the decorative throw pillows Carmela had piled onto the living room armchairs, making it impossible to sit anywhere comfortably. He'd have slashed the canvases decorating the dining room, bucolic landscapes that had hung at his in-laws' house—symbols of a bourgeoisie whose version of paradise was off-limits to brown people like him. With the seafood knife, he would have given his brother a nasty fright, a little nick just over his jugular vein. On his most recent visit, Ernesto had suggested that Ramón sell his house and move to an apartment to reduce his expenses, crudely pressuring his brother to pay back the loan as soon as possible.

"You're only three blocks from Avenida Insurgentes. You're sitting on top of a gold mine! Look, we can talk to my pal from the country club who's a big deal in the city government. He can get us a building permit for whatever you want—a high-rise, offices, commercial, a whorehouse. Construction companies would be lining up! They'll pay you in cash, you can take care of your bills and find an apartment somewhere nearby, no sweat."

Ramón was astounded by his brother's lack of tact. Was he really a talented businessman, or just a numbskull with a bit of luck? He remembered how, when they were boys, he would play with toy soldiers, masterminding complex battles commanded by famous historical generals, while Ernesto crawled around on the roof and cooed like a pigeon. "You're such an idiot," Ramón had said countless times to his younger brother. And now the brilliant military strategist owed the idiot more than a million pesos.

During those months, Ramón's only comfort was that Dr. Aldama, despite his aloof and unpleasant nature, had managed to get him admitted to the National Cancer Institute, where his chemotherapy and testing would be practically free of charge. To show his gratitude for this act of goodwill, Ramón wanted to get him a classy gift—perhaps a bottle of brandy, or better still, a case of Takemitsu knives. When she read his suggestion, Carmela reminded him that their credit cards were maxed out, and that with the meager income from his law firm, they could barely make it to the end of the month. Ramón's token of appreciation would have to wait.

The first chemotherapy cycle took place at the end of February, with moderate doses of the vincristine-actinomycin-cyclophosphamide trio—a classic formula of the old guard. Aldama availed himself of a military metaphor to explain to Ramón and Carmela that he'd decided to stick with the foot soldiers of chemo, as long as it wasn't necessary to call in the motorized infantry.

The second cycle, which now included ifosfamide and interferon, began to lay waste to the battleground. Ramón lost clumps of hair and broke out in cold sweats, and every orifice in his body burned. He felt miserable and ashamed as he wrapped himself up in scarves and hats, squeezed drops in his eyes, rubbed balm on his lips and cream on his anus—things he deemed more appropriate for old ladies and homosexuals. He was crushed by the weight of his debts. There was no way to pay them without losing his principal asset: the house where he was now wilting and fading away. A thousand square feet of real estate in a residential neighborhood—the only thing that was his to leave to his children.

With no villain to put on trial, he punished himself. I'm no use anymore, he would conclude as he struggled to read the documents Carmela submitted to him for approval, his mind clouded by the fog of chemotherapy. He would rather feign a headache than admit that he couldn't remember which client or case she was talking about.

He flirted with the idea of suicide. A bullet to the roof of the mouth—a surefire exit. Paulina would miss him most, his vulnerable, doting daughter, who sat with him watching TV and eating cookies. "Shall I put some cookies in the blender for you?" Her fond attentions served both as a comfort and a bitter reminder of his impotence. If he were to end his torment, he would have to make sure that Carmela didn't sell the house to pay off their debts. But how? Their marriage gave them joint tenancy with right to survivorship. Ergo, he should divorce Carmela and sign his part of their property over to her, so that after his death, she wouldn't be legally bound to the creditors of the deceased. At his miserly brother's behest, Ramón had signed an IOU for a million pesos. That much was true. And after the debtor's suicide, what would happen? Exactly what that ungrateful asshole had proposed all along: the house would be sold. But guess what? Unfortunately, before blowing his brains out, the deceased divorced the defendant and signed the title to the house at such and such address over to her. The debtor therefore died with no assets to be seized. Tough shit, asshole. You're fucked.

"And what are you grinning about?" Carmela asked him.

We're getting a divorce, thought Ramón, thrilled with his plan and determined to see it through. Carmela had bought a notebook for him to write down his messages, but Ramón could almost never remember where he'd left it and had to resort to random scraps of paper to communicate. He picked up an electricity bill, and wrote:

I want to sign my part of the house over to you, to avoid any trouble. I want the title to be in your name.

"Stop thinking about that. The doctor said this is an adjuvant treatment and there's nothing to worry about right now. The house belongs to us, and we're going to leave it to our children. Why do you want to worry about all of that?"

I don't want Ernesto to do anything to you. If something happens to me and I can't pay him back, I don't want him to bother you. I wouldn't put it past him!

"Please stop thinking about that. I've already told you, he said we don't need to worry. It doesn't matter, even if it takes us ten years. And we'll have paid him back before you know it."

Ramón couldn't think about anything else. He didn't want to pay up. Since he'd been diagnosed with cancer, since he'd lost the use of his words, he also felt that he was no longer subject to the law, that the obligations it dictated no longer applied to him. He hadn't accrued his debt voluntarily, nor had Ernesto amassed his fortune by honest means. The fairest solution, though it was impossible to say so, was for Ernesto to cover his brother's medical bills. If he wasn't willing to do so of his own accord, Ramón would force him to do so by killing himself. But it wasn't his debts that would drive him to suicide, like so many cowards in the peso crisis of '94; he was going to make his exit for the sake of his dignity, and for his family, who didn't deserve the burden of living with an invalid.

Promise me you won't pay him back if I'm not here, Ramón pleaded.

"You're so stubborn," said Carmela.

The next evening, she summoned the children to the kitchen and said, "We need to keep an eye on your dad. He seems really depressed."

Mateo felt guilty for not spending more time with his father, but whereas before the cancer Ramón had been unpleasant, now he was insufferable. Since he took ill, his father's expansive personality had become a black hole that sucked the energy out of everything around it. That was why Paulina ate so much, Mateo thought, to recover the strength sapped by her father's company. Mateo had always suspected that Ramón despised him for being so different from him, so shy and sullen.

"We should throw him a birthday party," Paulina said excitedly.

"He's not going to like that idea," said Mateo.

"Then we'll have to persuade him," said Carmela, knowing that this celebration might be the last. "Good idea, Pau."

Carmela turned toward the fridge and looked San Peregrino in the eye. The saint looked pleased.

10

After two weeks without going to therapy, Eduardo arrived at Teresa's house in a surgical mask. He'd come down with bronchitis.

"It's my mother's fault. She brought a virus home from her office. That place is like a medieval orphanage—they've never even heard of soap. I've asked her a thousand times to wash her hands when she comes home, not to touch her face, and to use the hand sanitizer I bought her." Eduardo had incorporated into his discourse the typical structures of a domineering mother. "As soon as she started coughing, I asked her to go to a hotel. She totally lost it. I tried to explain that if she stops touching her face with her hands, the probability of contagion is reduced by eighty percent. It's so easy, and she won't do it. So, obviously, she infected me. Oh, but she says she didn't have the flu—she's just allergic to the cold. I mean, where did she get the idea that the cold causes allergies? Allergies are a reaction to . . ."

Teresa's mind wandered from what Eduardo was saying.

She felt a visceral urge to interrupt him, to confront him with his fundamental need to break free from his neurotic prison. But Eduardo kept talking incessantly, caressing the squeaky-clean bars of his cell. And what about her? Wasn't her house a prison, albeit outfitted with a psychoanalytic practice and a clandestine marijuana greenhouse? She'd found her life's mission in providing psychoanalysis and psycho-tropic treatment to cancer patients, but it filled her days with a gruesome amount of suffering. Should she take a vacation? A break from her appointments could upset her psychological balance. She didn't want to go back to the depression she'd suffered when young, chain-smoking and popping sleeping pills like they were candy. Somehow, cancer had saved her from her innate sorrow; it led her to try medical marijuana, join a support group, spend whole days in bed reading Your-cenar, Butler, and Roudinesco. Thanks to cancer she'd met her best friend Rebeca, and thanks to it, too, she'd discovered her true vocation.

Meanwhile, Eduardo kept railing against his mother.

"Every five minutes, she tells me not to exaggerate. She spent all week telling me nothing was wrong and I should go to class, but right now is exactly when it's most dangerous to expose myself. Apart from that, I'm thinking of other people. Even though I'm almost better, I'm still a vector of disease. The illness has evolved to be contagious before and after the symptoms appear in the host."

Eduardo had a psychosomatic coughing fit.

"When do you think you'll go back to class?" Teresa asked him.

"Monday. Maybe."

Teresa stayed silent. Eduardo continued.

"I'm thinking of switching to online courses."

"You told me they weren't as good."

"They aren't, but what's the point of being enrolled at the university, if I have to miss so many classes? I'm already behind on everything this semester."

"Can't Emilia help you catch up?" Teresa realized at once that she'd spoken the words of an interfering mother. She was the analyst, but her unconscious refused to accept it.

Eduardo paused for a long time before answering. Teresa couldn't believe how clumsy she'd been. No wonder the Lacanian school still had its followers: it was the only one that prevented its adherents from giving away just how pedestrian the mind of the analyst was, how vulnerable to the patient's influence, to the projection of its own fears and desires.

"Am I that obvious?" said Eduardo, annoyed.

"How so?" asked Teresa, regaining her professional demeanor.

In an instant, Eduardo had been transformed into a normal young man with a crush on a classmate, a classmate he knew nothing about, aside from her appearance, her insightful comments in class, and the stiff manner in which she'd approached him three months earlier to ask for his notes. Oh, but there was one more detail, a psychological hook: Emilia never greeted anyone with a kiss. Eduardo watched her closely before and after class, in the corridors and classrooms, and in the literature department courtyard; whenever anyone tried to greet her with a kiss on the cheek, she held out her hand to stop them, polite and distant, with a glacial smile. Eduardo didn't know if this admirable behavior was due to hygienic reasons—phobias, in fact, like his own—or if it was an expression of blunt rebellion, a way of communicating her contempt for social norms.

Eduardo was flustered and squirmed on the couch as he spoke, tangling his sheet and dirtying it with the soles of his shoes. Teresa couldn't decide whether to continue her psychoanalytic exploration of the recesses of his psyche, or to play Cupid and offer him practical tips for pursuing a girl. If Eduardo rushed into trying to attract her and failed, the setback could harden his neurotic defenses and activate the explosive misogyny lodged in the hearts of all unsatisfied men.

"What do you think?" he asked Teresa.

"What do you want to do?" she answered quickly. They were almost out of time.

"I don't know. It would suck to find out she's a Mormon and doesn't kiss because it's a sin or she's afraid she'll get pregnant."

"Do you think that's why?"

"No, actually she's really smart. I just don't know how to talk to her."

"Shall we continue next week?"

Eduardo got up from the couch, bundled his sheet into a plastic bag, put on his surgical mask, and went on his way.

11

When he awoke on the Friday morning of his birthday, Ramón didn't suspect that by the end of the day he'd be involved in the perpetration of two federal crimes. The first was committed by Elodia, who arrived at work in the company of an *Amazona oratrix*, an endangered species of parrot whose trade was punishable under Article 420, Sections IV and V, of the Federal Criminal Code.

"Happy birthday to yooouuu, happy birthday to yooouuu, happy birthday, Señor Handsome, happy birthday to yooouuu!"

She burst into the study, where Ramón was watching TV, carrying a birdcage inside which, hunched on a thin perch, sat a half-bald parrot with a yellow head and grimy claws. "Look what I brought for your birthday!" she said, brandishing the cage like a war trophy.

She set the cage down on the desk. The parrot was young and male, and looked like it'd had a tough time at the gritty Sonora Market. The poor creature was dazed from the stress of being jolted around on the hour-long bus ride with Elodia. It also looked sick and malnourished. Ramón took an immediate liking to the ungainly bird.

Elodia was in high spirits.

"They told me this one's very chatty, that's why I picked him." A smell of soggy newspaper and rancid tomatoes wafted from the cage. "We'll teach him to call me whenever you need anything."

It was a harebrained idea. Unlike dogs, parrots had never acted as service animals. A dog could guide its blind owner, but a parrot couldn't possibly act as a mouthpiece for a mute. Yet, despite the gift's absurd nature, Ramón was grateful. He didn't care that parrot trafficking was illegal. As each day passed, he grew more indifferent to the law.

"I've been teaching him my name," Elodia said, turning to face the parrot. "Say Elodia! E! lo! dia! Elodia! Or shall we teach him to call me 'Elo,' like Paulina?"

Ramón closed his eyes and shrugged to indicate that it didn't matter.

"Do you like him?" asked Elodia, who had blown all her savings on the bird.

Ramón assured her sincerely that he did. The parrot seemed gifted with an intelligence far greater than should normally fit in such a small head. His wide eyes scrutinized his surroundings warily. Ramón felt flattered by the interest with which the bird contemplated him.

"They told me he's still young, that's why he's missing some feathers, and he's hurt himself with all his playing. But he'll get better."

Ramón was doubtful. Perhaps, like him, the parrot was

suffering from a devastating illness. Its featherless chest and bloody toes might be the result of a nefarious dose of veterinary chemotherapy. Its cage was cramped like a hospital bed and its drinking trough was empty. Ramón was well acquainted with the untamed stallion of convalescent thirst. He opened the cage door and removed the plastic container. The parrot remained on its perch.

"Look!" Elodia exclaimed in surprise. "He really likes you. I have to cover my hand so the little shrimp doesn't bite me."

Ramón handed her the container so that Elodia could go to the kitchen and fill it with water. He was left alone with the parrot. To break the ice, he said in his mind: You look almost as lousy as I do.

———

When Carmela finished showering and came down to breakfast, she found a mangy bird in the study.

"Where did that parrot come from?" she asked, scandalized, as she walked into the kitchen.

"That's the birthday present I brought for Señor Martínez," Elodia said proudly.

Ramón was in a celebratory mood, about to finish his second smoothie of the morning.

"Oh, but Elodia, what a shame," Carmela answered. "The doctor told us we can't have pets in the house while Ramón is in treatment. He could get an infection. The poor thing doesn't look very well, either," she said, feigning pity. "He looks like he's been run over."

Ramón took his wife's last comment personally, as if she were alluding to him. Furthermore, in his opinion, a parrot didn't count as a pet. Pets were mammals that licked their own assholes and sniffed at the excrement of other pets; pets were cats that scratched the furniture and marked their territory with urine. A parrot was more of an ornamental bird, more closely related to houseplants than to dogs, cats, or hamsters, those frightful rodents that Paulina had insisted on keeping as a little girl, until one of them had babies and the other one gobbled them up.

"If you like, I'll take him to the vet," Elodia answered defensively, "to see if he's sick."

"It's not a question of whether he's sick. It's just that Ramón's immune system is weak right now, and anything like that could be bad for his health," Carmela said. She turned to her husband. "Don't go into the study until it's been vacuumed and aired out." Ramón gestured an emphatic "Bah," and Carmela concluded with an order to the maid. "Will you please take it out to the patio right away?"

Elodia obeyed grudgingly. Ramón also failed to disguise his annoyance.

"It can't be helped," Carmela said, putting an end to the matter. "I feel bad for her, but we can't take any risks. Listen, this afternoon Elodia and Paulina are going to cook for your party. You go on up to the bedroom so it'll be a surprise, okay?"

Ramón had been opposed to the party, which, given the scarcity of potential guests, would in fact just be a small gathering with Ernesto and his family, and some friends Ramón and Carmela had dinner with a few times a year. Ramón had poured every ounce of his social energy into cultivating relationships with his clients, and little by little had ended up without any close friends. Carlos was the only one who'd shown any real concern for Ramón's well-being after the surgery.

Carmela sat down next to Ramón and quickly began to eat the fruit Elodia served her each morning. Elodia soon came back into the kitchen through the door that led to the patio.

"I put him outside. He looked like he was cold, poor little thing."

Under no circumstances was Ramón going to allow Elodia to take the parrot away. Since becoming mute, he'd learned to develop his arguments fully before bothering to look for a pen and paper to express them. He decided to wait until Carmela came home from the office, then confront her with his decision to keep the absurd and generous gift.

At midday, Ramón went out to the back patio for the first time in several weeks. The cage rested on the garden table, a round wrought-iron monstrosity shaded by a sun-bleached umbrella. The parrot stood on its perch. Its hunched posture made it look meek, as if ashamed of its bedraggled appearance.

Ramón pulled one of the heavy chairs out from under the table and sat down. He lifted a hand toward the bars, and the parrot gave a hop, determined to defend itself. It's okay, don't get in a flap. Between its sharp jaws, the parrot had a dark and bulging tongue.

You have the face of a Benito, thought Ramón. I'm going to call you Benito Juárez, after the president. He was the true father of the nation. Hidalgo and Morelos were just a couple of bickering priests. And then there's that fucking Madero, a rich kid from Coahuila who liked to commune with the dead. Juárez was pragmatic. He knew the country needed to move forward. He reformed the legal system and put the clergy and the military in their place—he did a fuckload of things. That was a real revolution, not like when all those caudillos rose up against Díaz, what a shitshow. These days they say Juárez was a traitor, but if he hadn't cut a deal with the gringos, we'd have been stuck with the Europeans. What would you have done? He was a brave motherfucker. Can you imagine what it meant back then for a Zapotec Indian to be president? I'm telling you, the guy had balls. Some people complain about how he had Maximilian shot. But what the hell did they want him to do with a guy who went around calling himself emperor of Mexico? Fine him and send him on his way? People don't have the slightest fucking clue what it takes to run a country.

The parrot was intrigued by this human who, unlike all the others it had met, didn't overwhelm it with noise and gestures. There was something comforting about his discreet gaze and total silence. Gradually, it began to relax in the patio, surrounded by bushes and flowerpots. Once it had grown used to Ramón's presence, it demonstrated its cheerfulness with one of the phrases it knew.

"Son of a bitch!" it squawked in a shrill and nasal voice. "Son of a bitch!"

Ramón let out his first guffaw since the tumor had appeared on the scene. The mutant sound that emerged from his lips was more like a sea lion's territorial bark than a human expression of delight.

"What the fuck?" answered the parrot.

Ramón roared with laughter. The parrot reiterated its surprise at its companion's unexpected reaction.

"What the fuck?"

Little did Elodia know that the parrot had picked up a broad repertoire of obscenities at the market. When she heard its squawks, she stuck her head out of the kitchen window and saw Ramón convulsing in his chair. She ran out of the house in fright.

"Señor! What's the matter?"

Ramón gave her a wave to dispel her fears. He was fine. Better, in fact, than he'd been at any time since losing his ability to say the very things the parrot was screeching.

"Cocksuckeeerrrr!" the parrot declared just at that moment.

"Keep it down, baldy!" Elodia said. "If Señora Martínez hears you, we'll both be out on the street."

Ramón went inside and headed upstairs to take a shower. He was in a splendid mood. He even managed to look at himself in the mirror without disgust before stepping into the shower, where he lingered for a while to enjoy the stream of hot water, carefully scrubbing away the smell of sickness coating his skin. He combed the sparse fuzz left on his head with his fingers, shaved a metaphysical beard, and splashed himself generously with aftershave. His newest clothes were ten sizes too big, so he put on an outfit he'd kept from his youth, when his Saturday night fever hadn't yet been stamped out. He patted himself on the back for having defended those shirts and pants from Carmela, who'd tried several times to donate them to a local insane asylum.

Once dressed, he caught sight of himself in the mirror.

This time, the youthful provenance of his outfit made him look more haggard than ever—his cheeks gaunt, dark purplish circles under his sunken eyes. He looked like a mummy exhumed from the cemetery in Guanajuato. He imagined the fright his appearance would cause the guests at his birthday dinner. He deeply regretted that his family, especially his daughter, had been so determined to throw him a party. How could he get them to call it off? The option crossed his mind of pretending to faint. But the danger was that Carmela might call an ambulance and he would be carted off to the emergency room at a private hospital, where, in their effort to squeeze more money out of him, a team of vultures would even subject him to a pregnancy test. He fantasized about fleeing. He would take off in the car and check into a five-star hotel where no one could find him; he would send the family a message telling them not to worry. He would run himself a bubble bath, order room service, watch some porn, then sleep soundly, undisturbed by Carmela's snores; in the morning, he'd stuff himself at the breakfast buffet, steal the slippers, the soap, and the little bottles of shampoo. Elodia's voice demolished his happy reverie.

"Señor! Your smoothie is ready!"

———

As soon as Mateo and Paulina got home from school, Elodia pestered them to go out to the patio and see her gift for their father. Her goal was to recruit them to plead the parrot's case and persuade their mother to let it stay in the house.

The parrot greeted them with suspicion. He clung to his perch and didn't utter a single expletive.

"Heinous," said Mateo.

"Ew, gross," said Paulina.

Neither showed any enthusiasm. Paulina asked what was for lunch.

"Noodle soup and roast chicken fillets," said Elodia, discouraged by the children's indifference to this new member of the household. "I've been in a rush to get the house ready for the party."

"When are we making dessert?" asked Paulina.

"As soon as you're done eating."

While Mateo and Paulina ate their soup, Elodia continued to lobby in the parrot's favor.

"You should've seen how happy that parrot made your dad. But now your mom says he can't keep it. Your dad was so disappointed. In my house we had chickens, turkeys, and dogs. They were all over the place. One time, we were raising a hog for San Bartolo—"

"What's that?" asked Paulina.

"A most miraculous saint, one of Jesus's disciples."

"No, the hog."

"Oh, it's a kind of pig, and they're not dirty like everyone says, they just have really dry skin. But it's true they'll eat just about anything, even your poop . . ."

"Yuck, Elo," said Paulina.

"So, tell us what happened," said Mateo.

"Ah, well, we were fattening him up for the fiesta and then it starts hailing, but so hard that the hailstones looked like guavas this big. We were afraid the pig would be killed by the hail, so we brought him inside. And he was fine, just like a dog. Everyone stroked him and no one got sick. How's a parrot going to be any worse?"

"I'm going to check online," said Paulina. "But I'm not into the idea. Daddy's really weak right now."

"I know," said Elodia, disheartened. "But you look it up and see what it says."

———

When Carmela came home, dinner was already prepared: cream of carrot soup, ground beef casserole, and chocolate pudding, soft-textured foods that Ramón could eat without too much trouble. The table was already set—crystal wine glasses, sparkling silverware, cloth napkins, and fine china. After a swift inspection, Carmela determined that the meat was undercooked, the sauce too thin, and the pudding too heavy. Numerous fingerprints besmirched the glasses and insolent knives lay with their blades facing out from the plates, which had gathered dust during their long sojourn in the display case.

Ramón found her rearranging the table settings. He handed her a statement in which he set forth in detail the reasons he had decided to keep the parrot. Firstly, he thought that to return it would be an affront "to our faithful household helper." Secondly, he thought they could entrust the bird's care to their children, "thus encouraging their sense of duty and responsibility, such an important aspect of their education." Finally, he was afraid the parrot salesmen would not accept its return, as a result of which the creature would end up living in deplorable conditions at Elodia's house. "It's a thousand times better for us to keep him here, where we can be sure he stays clean and healthy, than for the poor creature to get sick at Elodia's house, where she doesn't have the resources to care for him, and from whom I might then very well catch a more dangerous illness." Ramón omitted the main reason he wanted to keep the parrot—that he liked it—since it seemed improper for a grown man.

Rather than persuading Carmela, the letter only strengthened her resolve. She answered him in a whisper so that Elodia wouldn't hear from the kitchen.

"We'll pay her if she can't take it back. She can give it to her children, or to someone else who wants it."

I want it, thought Ramón.

"I'm sorry if she's offended, but we can't take this kind of risk just to keep the maid happy. That's all we need."

Let's ask the doctor and then decide, Ramón wrote in a conciliatory hand. His mutism had subdued his authoritarian impulses.

"All right, we'll ask him, but she'll have to take it away for the moment. I'm terrified you could catch an infection."

He can stay outside.

"That bird looks sick."

And I don't?

"Why are you pointing at yourself? That's irrelevant. And anyway, who's going to take care of it on weekends? I'm not taking any chances. What if it bites us?"

Ramón prepared to write down another objection.

"Please don't keep arguing, it's getting late. If the doctor gives his permission, then we'll tell Elo to bring it back."

It was exhausting to argue when he couldn't exercise his right of reply. Ramón gave up. So as not to witness the parrot's departure, he went upstairs and shut himself in his room.

He looked at himself again in the mirror. His face would inspire pity and disgust. He felt he could now relate to the people in photos of Nazi concentration camps, baffled and emaciated survivors, among mass graves overflowing with corpses. He knew the comparison was disproportionate, but he couldn't get the absurd feeling out of his mind that, like them, he was a prisoner and a ghost.

Carmela interrupted his narcissistic torture.

"As soon as I finish my makeup, I'm going to have to go buy some more tomato sauce. I hope there's time."

She sat down at the dressing table and began to outline her eyes. As he watched Carmela gradually transformed by eyeliner and mascara, Ramón had a revelation: his cadaverous appearance could be concealed with makeup. Was he about to celebrate his fiftieth birthday in drag? As long as the guests didn't see his ashen skin, the dark circles beneath his eyes, or his sunken cheeks, as long as they didn't feel sick at the sight of his face, or pity his sorry state, Ramón was willing, for one night only, to betray his self-image as a proud macho who looked down on unmanly affectations.

He picked up his notebook and opened it to where he'd written his arguments in defense of the parrot. He turned the page and paused, contemplating its blankness. He didn't want to sound anxious, or, worse still, effeminate. How could he ask her to make him up without impugning his virility?

He rehearsed the different options in his mind. Put a bit of makeup on me, would you? Could you give me some of that stuff to help me look less lousy? I look half dead, don't I? The ridiculousness of the situation prevented him from thinking clearly. Carmela had almost finished her own makeup. She was about to leave. Ramón wrote hurriedly:

I look really pasty. Can you put something on my face?

This approach allowed him to allude to the makeup without mentioning it explicitly, so he could wait for her to suggest it, apparently of her own accord. He handed her the notebook politely, stifling all the bitterness built up inside him over the incident with the parrot, and the fact that she was to blame for the dinner about to take place against his will.

"Don't worry," answered Carmela. "Who's going to notice?"

Everyone, thought Ramón, including himself. He had spent all day seeing himself through the eyes of others; the view was insufferable.

Put some cream on my face or something.

"It's going to take more than a cream to get rid of those dark circles."

Ramón looked toward the dressing table and raised what little was left of his eyebrows. Finally, she understood.

"You want me to make you up?" asked Carmela, amused by the prospect of putting makeup on a man who used Palmolive hand soap as shaving cream.

If he'd had the strength, Ramón would have blushed.

Would it be too obvious?

"I don't think so. You'd just need a little foundation and concealer. Do you want me to do it for you?"

Ramón pretended to be undecided for the sake of his dignity. Then he agreed.

"Okay!" she said eagerly. "Sit down here."

———

Ernesto arrived with his family and a bottle of barrel-aged tequila. Due to the stress on his liver caused by the chemotherapy, alcohol was strictly forbidden for Ramón; the sight of that elixir gave him a pang of sorrowful longing. His nieces got scared when they saw him, and Alicia had to push them toward him subtly to give him a kiss. She, for her part, had brought her brother-in-law a gift: a wooden plaque engraved with a cross, a dove, and a motto, a pearl of wisdom that read, "When you no longer have the strength to stand, kneel in prayer." Alicia had purchased this sadistic slogan at a bazaar selling handicrafts made by nuns. Ramón tried to process the atrocity she handed him.

"It's for you to put somewhere special," Alicia added.

In the trash can, thought Ramón, making no effort to hide his displeasure.

"What crawled up your ass? Don't you like our little gift?" Ernesto asked with his usual coarseness. "She's so stubborn. I told her, Ramón's a total heathen, but she paid no attention. What am I supposed to do? That's why I always bring booze."

"It's a lovely picture," Carmela intervened, wresting it from Ramón's atheist hands. "I think we'll hang it in the bedroom."

The tension dissipated among green olives, Chihuahua cheese cubes, ham roll-ups, and crispy pork rinds. Soon, Carlos and Laura arrived with a bottle of champagne, which Ramón also wouldn't be able to drink. Carmela took the bottle over to the fridge, where she came face-to-face with the beatific image of San Peregrino. She begged the saint to banish discord from her home that evening.

Meanwhile, in the living room, an awkward silence hung in the air, which Carlos finally broke with a simple yes-no question, the only kind Ramón could answer.

"Do you remember Manolo Icaza, from our procedural law class?"

Ramón remembered him perfectly. He was a blond and immature version of the matinée idol Mauricio Garcés. He'd been admitted to the UNAM thanks to his prominent family, who wielded considerable influence in the university administration. His academic performance was substandard and his ability to attract women superhuman.

"Well, wait till you hear this. It's not out of the bag yet, but he's on the short list for the Supreme Court."

"Is he a real hotshot or something?" Ernesto asked, while Ramón wrote in his notebook: *He married one of President Alemán's granddaughters. Otherwise he'd never even have made it to municipal clerk.*

"He's married to one of Miguel Alemán's granddaughters," said Carlos. "They own half the state of Veracruz, imagine the power they must have. He was a dunce. Isn't that right, pal?" he asked Ramón, who passed up the opportunity to say something redundant, and crossed out the message he'd just finished writing. He agreed, disheartened.

"He was a playboy," Carlos went on. "He passed all his classes by inviting the professors to his beach house in Acapulco. I've heard he used to throw some really wild parties. Women, drugs, movie stars."

Ramón began to write down a scandalous anecdote involving Manolo Icaza and the daughter of Ignacio Burgoa Orihuela, the university's most formidable law professor in those days. By the time he'd finished writing the story, the others had moved on to discussing the glitzy lifestyles of politicians, and Ramón realized that once again he'd been wasting his time. He dashed off a couple of lines and passed the notebook to Carmela to read them aloud. Carmela waited for Carlos to finish slandering the governor of Chihuahua, then said, "Let's see. Ramón says here, 'What we need is an Anti-corruption Officer, but not elected by the Senate.'"

Just then, Ernesto's cell phone rang. He answered it then and there, and his booming voice distracted everyone present. No one responded to Ramón's remark. His mood, already soured, began to fester.

When Ernesto deigned to end his call, the conversation resumed along well-trodden paths that ended in pools of expectant silence while Ramón wrote down what he wanted to say. Ernesto downed his fourth tequila of the evening and asked for a blackboard to fast-track his brother's contributions, since otherwise they'd end up having dinner at three in the morning. No one laughed. Alicia tried to control the damage with baseless flattery.

"With these delicious hors d'oeuvres, we aren't in any hurry."

"We have to be practical," said Ernesto. "Although, frankly, that isn't your strong point. You lawyers make everything so fucking complicated."

"Keep that up and I'll have to sue you," Carlos joked.

Ernesto seemed on the verge of making another stupid remark, but Carmela preempted him by asking everyone to come to the table. On his way from the living room to the dining room, Ramón thought about Carlos and Ernesto's exchange. Libel, slander, and calumny had been decriminalized at the federal level several years earlier. That abolition was irrefutable proof of just how devalued words had become; their use for defamatory purposes merited only the paltry seventeen thousand pesos' compensation recommended in the ridiculous Law for the Protection of the Right to Privacy, Honor, and Reputation.

As host and birthday boy, Ramón was seated at the head of the table, where it was easy to be cut off from the conversation. Carmela sat to his left, and Ernesto to his right. His brother was determined to be the center of attention and told a string of off-color jokes. Along with the difficulty of fishing for the croutons in the carrot soup, this caused the guests to forget to turn toward Ramón, and little by little he ended up completely excluded.

A silent witness, Ramón dined on a small portion of soup, and a plate of ground beef that Carmela served him separately. Without a tongue to push the food between his teeth and back into his throat, chewing was a slow and laborious process. He had to tilt his head back to swallow and let gravity do the rest. By the time everyone else had finished, Ramón still hadn't eaten even half of his beef. He signaled dishonestly to Carmela that he was full, and asked her to remove his plate.

Paulina and Mateo, who'd had dinner in the kitchen with

Ernesto's daughters, helped clear the table. A few minutes later, Carmela turned out the lights and Paulina emerged from the kitchen with a glass dish of chocolate pudding. In the middle burned a single candle, long and thick like a paschal candle, tilted to one side in the viscous cream. Once Paulina had placed the dessert in front of her father, Carmela straightened the candle with a finger, and signaled for everyone to start singing. Ramón endured the cacophony, his gaze fixed on the tongue of fire that symbolized his fifty years. It was a precise and fickle symbol, surrounded by noise and darkness. Applause. Paulina told him to make a wish and blow out the candle. Ramón imagined the assembled company crying at his funeral. He blew out the candle with a desultory puff and had a coughing fit. Happy birthday.

The sight of the dollop of pudding on his plate made Ramón think of the shapeless feces of a dyspeptic dog.

"Here's your slice," Carmela joked as she served the dessert. The guests smiled out of obligation.

Carlos fetched the bottle of champagne he'd brought, poured it into the clean glasses, and proposed a toast. Carmela whispered to Ramón to remind him that he couldn't drink. She told him to pretend to take a sip, and that she would finish his glass for him.

"My dear Ramón," said Carlos. "My wife and I sincerely hope that you continue to be an example of strength and bravery to us all. May this year bring you many blessings. Cheers!"

"Cheers," everyone mumbled.

Ernesto, who was now thoroughly inebriated, quaffed his champagne in a single gulp.

"Moët Pérignon. A taste of the high life!" he said.

Ramón noticed the mistake immediately: the bottle Carlos had brought was Moët & Chandon, which was much cheaper than Dom Pérignon, the princess of all champagnes. Ernesto's mix-up of the names might have been an innocent mistake, but Ramón was convinced that he'd done it on purpose to embarrass his friend.

Ernesto leaned across the table, lifted the bottle of champagne, and emptied it into his glass, which overflowed with bubbles. Ramón saw Alicia wince, mortified by the speed of her husband's drinking. She scolded him inaudibly. Ernesto replied by raising his voice.

"Leave me alone, goddamn it! You won't even let me enjoy some Moët Pérignon!"

Ramón relished the degrading spectacle his brother was causing.

"I think we should be going," Laura said to Carmela. Her tone betrayed proxy embarrassment, a quintessentially Mexican variety of commiseration.

Carlos agreed firmly, perhaps offended by the supposed joke about the "Moët Pérignon."

"Don't leave yet," protested Ernesto. "The night is young. We're celebrating my brother's birthday. He's even dolled himself up for you!"

At the beginning of the evening, Ramón hadn't noticed any unusual reactions to his face, so he'd relaxed in the belief that Carmela's subtle handiwork on his complexion had gone undetected. But now no one could fail to notice. He was wearing makeup, and Ernesto's declaration made it all the more humiliating. Ramón tried to muster some obscenities to attack his brother, at least in his mind—to express his mute rage by riddling Ernesto with silent insults—but nothing, not a single word, responded to the call of hatred. All profanity escaped him, crowding onto the tip of his absent tongue.

Alicia scolded her husband again under her breath.

"But he looks so adorable," Ernesto answered back in an effeminate voice.

No, not a single word deigned to come to his aid. Ramón leapt up from his chair, grabbed the champagne bottle by the neck, and smashed it over his brother's head in a single, fluid motion. Ernesto barely managed to cover his face. The bottle's heel struck him squarely on the forehead. Attempting to flee from the attack, he crashed facedown onto the table. Alicia shielded him with a protective embrace.

The bottle trembled in Ramón's right hand. Carmela ordered him to let it go. Ramón turned to her, disobedient, with the eyes of a cornered lion.

Paulina and the girls, who'd been watching a movie, came running out of the study when they heard the commotion and were met with the sight of a bourgeois parody of a bar brawl. Ernesto bellowed threats and insults and struggled to sit up straight while Alicia and Carlos kept him pinned to his chair. Laura and Carmela held on to Ramón by the arms, attempting to push him toward the kitchen.

"Give me my money!" Ernesto demanded, frothing at the mouth with rage. "Hand it over right now, you fucking faggot!"

"Shut up," Alicia begged.

Laura and Carmela tussled with Ramón, who tried to break free from their grip.

"You're going to die!" Ernesto predicted, revived by adrenaline. "Your karma's going to catch up with you, fucking loser!"

Alicia tried to gag Ernesto and he bit her by mistake. Her shrill cry pierced through Mateo's headphones; he was shut in his room, oblivious to the kerfuffle. He ran downstairs and found the girls bawling, two of the women consoling them, and Carlos trying to drag his uncle Ernesto, who wouldn't stop shouting, to the front door.

"Get out here, you fucking asshole! We'll see who pays for your funeral!"

Ramón listened from the kitchen, panting and cornered against the stove by his wife. He felt more satisfied by the minute with what he'd done. He'd just committed a crime listed in Article 289 of the Federal Penal Code. He felt extraordinarily pleased with himself.

The cries became more and more distant, then faded completely. Laura informed them from the other side of the kitchen door that everyone had left.

Carmela poured a glass of water and handed it to Ramón. There was no need for the gesture. Her husband hadn't been driven into a rage by his thirst, nor was it time for his medication. The glass of water was there to fill an unbearable void. Ramón accepted it and took a sip. He tilted his head back and felt the insipid, cool water trickle inside him. When he looked down, his eyes met Carmela's baffled gaze.

What the hell are you looking at?

PART II

Illness is not a metaphor, and . . . the most truthful way of regarding illness—and the healthiest way of being ill—is one most purified of, most resistant to, metaphoric thinking. —Susan Sontag

12

The Aldamas arrived at the sumptuous Church of the Immaculate Conception shortly before the ceremony began. They were attending the wedding out of duty to the bride's father, a pulmonologist who often referred his patients to Joaquín Aldama's private practice.

The doctor had spared no expense. The church was festooned with ribbons, bows, and floral arrangements. A troupe of bored paparazzi swarmed around snapping pictures of guests in tuxedos and bow ties or evening dresses. Here and there, the occasional renegade clashed with the surroundings in a clownish tie or a provocative miniskirt. The Aldamas adhered strictly to protocol. Joaquín loathed any outfit that didn't include a white coat, an indispensable piece of armor for his superiority complex. He wasn't the only uncomfortable one in the church. Tight corsets, ill-fitting rented suits, high heels, minuscule purses, caked-on makeup, professional hairdos, constant sweat, and postprandial drowsiness afflicted the majority of the guests bused in for the occasion. They took their pews according to an invisible gradient of familiarity: the closer their ties to the bride and groom, the closer they sat to the front of the church.

The Aldamas sat in the third row from the back, beneath the choir, where a chamber orchestra massacred Mendelssohn's "Wedding March" as the priest and bridal party processed down the aisle. The quality of their playing led Joaquín to surmise that the musicians belonged to a deaf-mute student symphony.

Once the March had ended and the ceremony began, Joaquín passed the time pondering Ramón's rhabdomyosarcoma. According to Luis Ramírez's animist metaphor, the tumor's cells behaved "like a bunch of fucking socialists," toiling with rare altruism on behalf of their neighboring cells, arranging themselves into little cavities like alveoli, and secreting chemicals that promoted growth and vascularization. By virtue of this behavior, the rhabdomyoblasts had formed a round and vigorous tumor in the patient's tongue and were now multiplying into harmonious layers in the petri dishes that hosted them.

"Mea culpa, mea culpa, mea maxima culpa," the other guests recited, beating their chests unrepentantly.

Aldama stayed silent, lost in thought. Usually, the DNA of a malignant cell contained hundreds of pernicious mutations, but Luis Ramírez believed that the rhabdomyosarcoma was caused not by a large number of disorderly genes, but by the alteration of a decisive few, the minimum necessary to spark a disciplined and at the same time unruly process of cellular reproduction. If the pathologist's suspicions were confirmed, the genome of those cells would represent a catalog of mutations essential for carcinogenesis. Ramírez's enthusiasm was justified by the revolutionary consequences of such a discovery: a universal cure for cancer, the Holy Grail of oncology.

"Alleluia! Alleluia!" the least inhibited guests chanted as the priest prepared to read a popular episode from the Gospels.

"And as Jesus passed by," he began in a reverential drone that transported Joaquín back to his schooldays with the Marist priests, "he saw a man which was blind from his birth. And his disciples asked him, saying, 'Master, who did sin, this man, or his parents, that he was born blind?'"

Aldama imagined the unseeing man's clouded corneas and pictured him sitting beside the dirt road begging for alms. Jesus seized the chance to flaunt his ophthalmological talent in front of his followers. He spat on the ground, kneaded a small lump of clay, and used it to anoint the patient's eyes. But why would the all-powerful Son of God need to avail himself of an improvised salve to heal one of his children? Perhaps it was a prop he used for dramatic effect, or, in the best-case scenario, an excipient for the active components of his redeeming saliva.

The Gospel of John neglected to mention whether the clay was applied to the eyeballs or to the eyelids. Aldama preferred to believe that the dirt hadn't come directly into contact with the blind man's eyes. Jesus commanded his patient to go and wash in the Pool of Siloam. Once again, the advice seemed gratuitous. Jesus had all the resources he could possibly need to heal the blind man, so why send the poor wretch off in search of a pool?

"He went his way therefore, and washed, and came seeing. The neighbors therefore and they which before had seen him that he was blind, said, is this not he that sat and begged? Some said, This is he. Others said, He is like him: But he said, I am he."

Aldama knew very well that an ointment alone could never have cured congenital blindness. The patient's cerebral cortex would have lacked the necessary connections to process the information transmitted via the optic nerve. In response to the deluge of incoherent sensations, he would have suffered a fatal epileptic seizure at the edge of the pool. But that wasn't to be; the blind man came back from Siloam completely unfazed, and since it was Saturday, no one had anything better to do than escort him to the temple so that the Pharisees could witness the miracle. Needless to say, they were less than convinced, and cast him out of the temple for his sins. In the end, Jesus came again to the patient, and revealed the episode's apocalyptic meaning: "For judgment I have come into this world, so that the blind will see and those who see will become blind." What an obnoxious way to end a medical procedure. Hippocrates and Jesus would have had their differences.

"The Word of the Lord," the priest concluded, before closing the book and kissing its cover.

During the sermon, Aldama's mind wandered again. What would the genetic makeup be of the son of a Jewish girl and an all-powerful deity? Had the Holy Spirit fertilized Mary's egg, or had he in fact placed a divine zygote inside her, fashioned ex nihilo for the occasion by God himself?

If Catholic orthodoxy held that Mary was the mother of God, then surely she was more than just an incubator. God must have infused her with a breath of holy sperm containing twenty-three chromosomes, including the Y chromosome that made Jesus a boy. The other twenty-three were supplied by Mary's egg; these carried the genes that determined her son's physique, the color of his skin and eyes, the thickness of his lips, the shape of his nose. Could the Son of God have fallen victim to cancer? His Father's chromosomes must have endowed him with infallible tumor suppressor genes—the P53, the NF1, the BRCA1, and the BRCA2. He could have eaten all the sausages he liked, chain-smoked, frequented tanning salons, and handled radioactive waste, all without having to fear the malignancies normally associated with those risk factors. What a healthy life Jesus might have led, if he hadn't made so many powerful enemies.

Joaquín's rambling train of thought was interrupted by the recitation of the marriage vows: Regina and her betrothed promised to love one another and be faithful as long as they both should live.

During the consecration of the host and wine, Aldama's phone began to vibrate in his pocket. He peered at it discreetly to see who was calling, and recognized Mrs. Martínez's number. She had never called him before on a weekend. He worried it could be an emergency and decided to leave the church to take her call. "Let us proclaim the mystery of faith," he heard the priest say before the door closed behind him. Once outside, he took his phone out of his pocket and saw that she had already hung up. He quickly returned her call.

Mrs. Martínez apologized profusely for bothering him on a Saturday, but it was a highly sensitive matter. The night before, her husband had attacked his brother with a champagne bottle. "He lost his mind," she elaborated. Aldama wondered what kind of champagne his patient had used.

"I've made an appointment for Monday with a therapist with a good reputation," Mrs. Martínez went on. "She specializes in helping patients with cancer. I talked to her on the phone and she was very reassuring. She said she can help us and not to worry, but Ramón's being really stubborn about it. We've been trying to convince him all day, and he's flat-out refusing to go."

"Why did he assault his brother?" Aldama asked casually.

"My brother-in-law had a few too many drinks and was talking nonsense, and Ramón lost it and hit him over the head. If he hadn't been so weak, he'd have split it open."

"Do you want me to try and convince him?"

"No, absolutely not. He'd be furious if he knew I'd told you. No, the thing is that yesterday our cleaning lady gave him a parrot, and I said we couldn't keep it because of what you told us. Ramón got mad like he does about everything these days, and went on and on trying to persuade me, and I told him it was out of the question. Well, just now he handed me a note demanding that I call the cleaning lady and tell her to bring the parrot right back. I'm really stressed because of last night and I didn't think it through, so I said, if we bring back the parrot, will you agree to see a therapist? And he said yes. So now what do I do? I've been wondering what to do for hours, and he just fell asleep, so I thought I should call you and ask if there's any way we could keep it . . ."

Aldama was taken aback by her ridiculous story. On the one hand, he applauded his patient's outburst. Bashing a drunk on the head with a champagne bottle was an ingenious way of meting out justice. On the other, he was amused by the idea of a maid giving her employer a parrot, and his wife using it as a marital bargaining chip.

"The parrot isn't at your house?" the doctor asked, buying himself some time to consider the case.

"No, I asked her to take it away yesterday afternoon."

"All right," he said. "If you think that it'll make him agree to see the psychologist, let him keep it. But take it to the vet for a checkup, and make sure it stays outside the house."

"Isn't it too risky for him?"

"The most important thing right now is to make sure he's happy. We'll keep an eye on the situation."

"Thank you so much, Dr. Aldama. That really puts my mind at rest."

"Don't mention it."

They said goodbye. When he went back into the church, Esther had come back from taking Communion and was kneeling in front of the pew, dissolving the body of Christ on her tongue. He sat down beside her and thought about Mr. Martínez's case. He'd just read a study in the *Lancet* about the effects of mood on disease progression in patients undergoing chemotherapy. A diagnosis of depression significantly lowered the chances of recovery. The most important thing was for him to keep his spirits up; if giving him a parrot achieved that, then so be it.

The ceremony ended with a piece by Handel—"The Arrival of the Queen of Sheba," a selection symptomatic of the megalomaniacal enthusiasm afflicting the newlyweds. As they played, the orchestra reached a level of cacophony more befitting of a mariachi ensemble. Aldama imagined the great Baroque composer spinning furiously in his grave at Westminster Abbey. If he'd had a champagne bottle at hand, Joaquín would have used it to clobber the musicians over the head and deliver the world from that musical horror.

13

Beneath a fake four-thousand-watt sun, the marijuana plants were putting in extra hours of photosynthesis. It was Monday night. Teresa was calmly tending the plants with ripened buds. Her body was soaked in sweat and her hands were coated in sticky, psychoactive resin. She smiled. The scent alone was enough to induce a profound state of calm. She'd had an intense day of group therapy and individual sessions. She had met Ramón, whose involuntary silence was going to prevent her from treating him in an orthodox manner.

Their first meeting was taken up with Carmela's account of the particulars of her husband's case, from his paralyzed tongue to his vicious attack on his brother three nights earlier. According to Carmela's sketch of his character, Ramón was impatient, domineering, and narcissistic, had immense confidence in his own intellect, and was woefully out of touch with his emotions.

Ramón had contributed only a few curt phrases, which he wrote down in his notebook with annoyance. It was a tiresome way to communicate: first he had to write down what he wanted to say, then pass the notebook and wait for his interlocutor to read it. Since the free association of ideas, a pillar of the psychoanalytic method, was impossible under those conditions, Teresa suggested an unusual strategy: they would conduct their sessions online via chat, but in her office. The dynamic would involve each of them using a laptop; that way, Ramón could type his messages and she could read them as soon as he sent them, almost simultaneously. Though it might seem absurd to chat online while in the same room, Teresa wanted to be face-to-face with Ramón, to observe the nonverbal expressions of his subconscious, and respond to them in person, paying close attention to his body language.

Ramón didn't seem keen on the suggestion. Carmela, on the other hand, was enthusiastic, and immediately thought of asking their son to lend them his laptop and teach them to use it. She seemed convinced that they would be going to therapy as a couple, but Teresa soon clarified that she needed to work with Ramón alone, at least at first.

The only thing Ramón had written without being prompted was the question, *How much will it cost?* When he learned what she usually charged, he could hardly disguise his dismay. Carmela explained that they were in a tricky financial situation, and Teresa offered to charge them on a sliding scale. Once they had settled the price of the sessions, they agreed to meet at the same time the following Monday.

When she finished pruning the leaves, Teresa cut the stems already bearing ripened buds and gathered them into a bunch, taking care not to graze the parts that were richest in psychotropic resin. These buds would spend a couple of weeks drying in an adjacent storage closet, hanging upside down from a clothesline. Once dehydrated, the buds would be set to cure in glass containers, a process that would take six months and result in a potent and delicately flavored herb.

To provide marijuana to the many patients who sought her help, moved by the stories of others to seek an alternative remedy, Teresa needed to grow increasingly large amounts. The demand had almost outpaced her supplies, and also those of the hippie biologist in Tepoztlán who provided her with specialized soil and cannabis fertilizer.

She was convinced that marijuana would be legalized before long, and she trusted that then she could be open about her work and leave this worthy social endeavor in the hands of others. Until then, she would be forced to turn away more and more patients, telling them that they would have to obtain it by their own means, though this meant they would end up buying an inferior product in a market controlled by criminals.

For months, she'd been thinking about finding a business partner, but she didn't know anyone with the privacy, space, or commitment to service required for that work, which on top of everything was punishable with jail time. For the moment, she would have to keep working alone.

After her strenuous labor, she went down to bathe. The moment she stepped into the shower and felt the warm water's embrace was her favorite part of the day. She lathered herself with an ultra-soft sponge, beginning at the nape of her neck and working her way down her sagging flesh; she circled the scars on her chest, two blind smiles where her nipples had been. The suds amassed in her pubic hair, which grew thinner by the day. Teresa sat down on a plastic bench to wash her legs. She wasn't in any hurry. She treated her aging body with motherly care.

Her thoughts returned to Eduardo, the youngest of her psychoanalytic children. On Saturday, after several weeks of not mentioning the subject, Teresa had decided to ask if he'd heard from his classmate Emilia. Irritated by the question, Eduardo told her that they'd studied Latin together, and that he hadn't enjoyed it. Why? Because Emilia chewed the cap of her pen. That innocent oral fixation was a deal-breaker for Eduardo. How many bacteria must there have been on that chunk of plastic that Emilia removed with her hands from her pencil case, placed on the desk, then raised to her mouth? He hadn't spoken to her since.

Teresa decided to confront Eduardo with the roots of his phobia. She asked him if he'd had any dreams about Emilia.

"What?" he said defensively.

"What did you dream about?" she insisted, betraying the most sacred principles of her school of analysis.

"I don't want to talk about it," he said, alarmed.

Teresa nodded respectfully, but she knew Eduardo wouldn't be able to stand his lack of control over what she might imagine. In the end, he told her.

He dreamed about her all the time. Emilia wanted to kill him, but whenever she tried to, she was the one who died. He nearly always lay in a hospital bed. She would cut off his oxygen, and then she would suffocate. That was the strange thing. Whenever she tied the cord around his neck, she was the one who turned blue in the face; her eyes bulged and then she lost consciousness. He tried to save her, but it was impossible; she kept strangling him until she killed herself. "Please don't kill me," he would beg her, though she was always the one who died.

Teresa considered the possibility that the dreams had an erotic component and might even result in ejaculation. She didn't dare ask. Their sadomasochistic duality intrigued her. It was rare for both drives to be satisfied in the same fantasy. What tipped the balance in favor of the masochistic interpretation was the fear, the begging, the attempt to save Emilia. But what did she represent in the dream?

Eduardo had come up with a reasonable explanation for the manifest content of his nightmares. According to him, her attempt to kill him had to do with his fear of contagion. "If she tried to kiss me, I'd be so disgusted," he admitted. On the other hand, he was in love with her. She was brilliant, shy, and very pretty. She would make a wonderful partner, but Eduardo would not. He could have a relapse at any moment. "If we got married, she could hurt me, but I would do her a lot more harm. That's why she's the one who dies in the dream. I'm a ticking time bomb. I know I'm going to get cancer again, and I don't want anyone else to have to suffer because of me." Eduardo's noble feelings toward Emilia had confirmed his decision to stay single and celibate for the rest of his life, for the good of others.

The dream's latent content represented the paradox of the jouissance of the Other. From a man's perspective, a female object of desire was the perfect embodiment of Lacan's nonexistent Other. Elsewhere, the enigmatic psychoanalyst stated that the body was made to seek enjoyment in itself. Cancer's body: its jouissance would kill Eduardo, and at the same time self-destruct. He begged it not to kill him, but he couldn't live without it. A return to the years of leukemia, that perverse idyll: once again, that was the thrust of Eduardo's fantasy. The novelty was that cancer returned in the guise of a woman. The chest of a masochist, Teresa thought, always concealed a misogynist's heart.

The recurring dreams functioned as an unconscious defense against the threat Emilia brought into Eduardo's life. To be happy, to surrender to his infatuation and to the risk of a successful seduction, meant relinquishing the symbolic order that, though rife with neuroses and phobias, gave his life meaning. It was too dangerous to let go: if he failed to win Emilia's heart, to find in her an object that would fill the void of desire, he would be left alone facing the abyss, and then he would suffer a psychotic break—the psyche's desperate strategy for regaining its grip on reality. Eduardo's terrifying nightmares were his mind's attempt to shield itself from a devastating madness.

Teresa had to resign herself to the fact that it would be a long time before Eduardo could have a normal emotional or sexual relationship. Simply put, he would remain alone, completely alone, just like her. She thought also of herself and her own projected desire, her fantasy of one day bathing at night, in the knowledge that someone would be there to have dinner with her, climb into bed and embrace her, accepting the absence of her breasts. Good night, my love, said the silence, when Teresa turned out the light.

14

"What the fuck?" said Benito when he saw Ramón walk in wrapped in a colorful, fringed wool poncho.

Yeah, I know. I look like Chavela Vargas, thought Ramón. Look, it might be gay, but it keeps my legs warm, so knock it off. I found it sorting through some old clothes in the closet. My mother-in-law gave it to me for Christmas about fifteen years ago. She did it to fuck with me, obviously, to let me know she thinks I'm an Indian or a faggot or both. But I don't give a damn. The chemo's screwed up my temperature, my digestion, my dick . . . and all for nothing. Now they tell me it's spread to my lung. A couple of gray spots showed up on the X-ray. *See what happens when you smoke two packs a day, jackass?* I could tell that's what they were thinking, but I haven't smoked in twenty years, Benito. And anyway, smoking has nothing to do with it. The doctor told me that more than once. What happened to me is like getting hit by a stray bullet, or more like a natural disaster, because it's not even a case of negligence or misconduct. That's right, a natural disaster. But look what it's cost me. Look at the fucking ordeal it's putting me through. It came out of nowhere. And now they want to blast these spots on my lung with radiation. What do I tell them? "No, that's okay, thanks, I've decided to end it all"? Imagine the fuss they'd make. Carmela would send me to the loony bin—I wouldn't put it past her. No, Benito, I'm not afraid to die. What I'm afraid of is the shame of leaving my children out on the street. Say they cure this metastasis, then what am I supposed to do? Nobody gets how degrading this is for me. I make a living from words, from giving people a voice in front of the authorities so they can protect their rights, demand accountability, resolve conflicts . . . I represent my clients. I speak for them. If I'm mute, I'm not worth shit. I can't do my job, it's that simple. If you can't do your job anymore, step aside. There are people waiting for a space at the table, so they can eat. But me, the waiter brought me the check before I was done. It hurts, that's for fucking sure. Don't think I'm made of stone. I've done my share of crying when no one was around. But right now, I'm focusing on what comes next. Leaving a legacy, even if it's humble, even if it's not much, so I can go in peace. And that includes you, Benito. I'm going to get you an awesome cage. I don't have a cent to my name, but I've been figuring out how to make it happen. I've got a solid gold watch, Benito. A little reward I got myself when I won a big case. I have it upstairs, locked up in a drawer with my gun. It's a beaut, Benito, .32-caliber—more than enough to do the job. First gold, then lead. I'll send a message to a guy at the office and have him come over without telling Carmela. Go get this watch valued and sell it for me. It'll bring in a tidy sum. And with that in my pocket, I can get going. Three things: one, pay the registry and notary fees. I sign over the house, we seal the divorce, and it's a done deal. Two, your cage, obviously—extra-large, so you can live it up. And three, pay for my funeral. I want to leave everything in order. Hell, I'd pick out the coffin myself if I could. I'll take that one, the mahogany. Then I'll get my suit ironed. Hell, if I have enough left over, I'll even buy a set of those knives on TV for Elodia, just for kicks. And you know what else? I'll leave that asshole Ernesto a letter he'll never forget. You're a fucking loan shark. But I'm not killing myself to get out of paying you, I'm doing it because I won't stand for being treated like an invisible lump. I'm doing it for my dignity. If you had any idea what dignity was, you'd have said, "You know what, Ramón? Forget about paying me back. You did a lot for us. That money's yours—I owed it to you." But no, you don't have the basic decency. So tough shit. You've swindled a bunch of people, now it's your turn to get fucked. I witnessed your scams firsthand, remember. And it's no crime to steal from a thief, isn't that what they say? I'll leave the letter right there. What do you say, Benito? Even if he wants to use it as evidence, if I'm gone and there are no assets left to be seized, then he's completely fucked.

———

Elodia came out to mop the patio and enjoy Ramón's company. Benito welcomed her with a hearty, "Lick my balls!"—a phrase he'd been taught to squawk when there were women around.

"Keep it down, baldy," Elodia said.

Ramón was tired of hearing Elodia refer to Benito

indiscriminately as "parrot," "bird," "blondie," "baldy," or "foulmouth." He took this opportunity to write her a note.

The parrot's name is Benito, like President Juárez. That's what you call him.

"What a pretty name, Señor Martínez. Hello, Benito! Your name's Benito, that's what your daddy called you. All right, Benito, now stop cussing and tell me your name: BE-NI-TO! BE-NI-TO!"

Not again, Elodia. Leave him alone.

"I have a cousin called BE-NI-TO! He was a real gem. He left the village years ago. You have no idea how much he did for my dear mother when she was sick, before you helped us bring her here. He'd take water over to her house and deliver her flour, eggs, and milk. I called him my guardian angel, that's what he was."

There are still good people in the world, Ramón thought with unwarranted nostalgia. Elodia started mopping the terrace.

"But his sister Fidelia, God rest her soul. She was my youngest cousin, and the poor thing had a nasty end. The devil did his work on her daddy. That's what Benito told me one time when he was drunk and got all upset. He told me that when his daddy got frisky, he'd do things to her. Never mind that she was his daughter, she was a little girl. He liked his liquor, just like my children's father. Remember?"

How could I not remember, he almost killed you.

"And he was always lying in the street or passed out somewhere near his house a ways out of town, just behind some cornfields. And then one day, a few people saw him lying there taking a nap, and they left him right where he was, 'cause he'd get stubborn as a mule if they tried to drag him home. Well, the next morning, the sun comes up . . ." At this point in her story, Elodia stopped mopping and lowered her voice to a scandalized whisper. "And there he was, lying on the ground, but without a head! Back in those days, you never heard anything about narcos or cartels. It was a quiet village. So where was his head? Well, after a while someone said that a dog was guarding it and chewing on it. Can you believe that? So, they were about to kill the dog they said had ripped his head off, but just then a friend of my uncle's who lived next door said that the night before, he'd seen my cousin Benito go out holding a machete, and he said to himself, Where's he off to at this time of night? And then a little bit later he saw him come back by himself . . ."

A ballsy young man. I salute him.

"So, they went and rounded Benito up, and he didn't say a thing."

In these cases, thought Ramón, it's best not to make any statement at all.

"And what do you think happened next? His sister went to the authorities and said that she'd done it and she had the machete right there in a sack, all covered in blood. And then my cousin finally piped up and said that it wasn't true, that it had been him. And she said no, that she was the guilty one, and if not, then how come she had the machete, not him?"

It was just a matter of comparing their statements to identify the inconsistencies, thought Ramón.

"Why am I telling you all this, again?"

Ramón pointed at Benito's cage.

"Oh, right, my cousin. Well, they had them both in custody

in the village, and before they called the police, the local authorities asked the priest to try and get the truth out of them. Well, heaven knows what the priest said, but it turned out to be Fidelia who'd done it, and they took her away. My poor aunt was all by herself for the funeral. I was right there with her. And just when they were lowering the coffin into the ground, we start hearing a muffled knock, like on a door, and my aunt starts screaming, 'He's alive! Let him out! Let him out! He's alive!'" Elodia's cries ruffled Benito. "And she wanted them to open the coffin, but they refused. Somebody figured out that the head was loose, rolling around in there and smacking against the wood. They had to keep a close eye on my aunt, she wanted to go to the cemetery and dig up the grave, because she was convinced they'd buried my uncle alive. And my cousin, when he was released from custody, he was like a recluse, and then soon after that he disappeared. I figure he went north. And poor Fidelia, who knows what it was she got hooked on in jail, but one day she overdosed. The poor thing died in a prison in San Luis Potosí. Would you lift your feet just a bit, so I can mop underneath? There you go. Thanks."

15

There were around thirty-seven trillion cells in each of Joaquín Aldama's patients. He himself had as many, though he didn't dwell on this fact too often. A single defective cell in a trillion was all it took for a cancer. Given these odds, which only increased with longevity, it was hardly remarkable that the disease should exist and flourish in a world that was teeming with geriatrics. What surprised him was stepping out into the street and seeing so many healthy people. Good health wasn't a state of peace and harmony with the environment, as naturopathic quack healers proclaimed. In fact, it was quite the opposite—a fleeting victory over chaos, a balancing act on a tightrope stretched over an abyss of turmoil. The "health" touted on TV was the opium of a century of narcissists, an effective illusion for marketing vitamins, salads, and activewear, but useless for understanding the body's relationship to the world. Just like the plague and tuberculosis in other eras, cancer revealed this "natural balance" to be a gargantuan sham, the missing clothes of an emperor not only naked but wasting away. Like people, the cells of the human body were obedient subjects, but sometimes a young rebel broke away from the established order and reproduced; once its offspring were legion, they became a threat to the empire, and the oncologist and surgeon were called in to quash the insurrection. Thirty-seven trillion cells, for instance, answered to the name Ramón Martínez, and among them lived a band of renegades—millions, regrettably, in his left lung, despite the glossectomy and massive intravenous doses of blistering chemotherapy delivered in two-week cycles.

Now it was time, Aldama thought, to move on to experimental chemo and daily radiation. He regretted having to resort to such harsh treatment, but he had no choice. The patient's life and that of a promising study were both on the line. Ramón's genome could become the Rosetta stone of oncology, the key to deciphering the grammar of cancer, its internal logic.

Along with the pulmonary metastases, the institute had discovered an unprecedented mutation in the FOX01 rhabdomyoblast gene. The gene normally functioned, among other things, as a fatty tissue regulator and tumor suppressor. Aldama suspected that this defective variety of FOX01 was involved as much in the Martínez family's predisposition to obesity as in the mysterious genesis of that childhood tumor.

The discovery would merit a privileged place in international medical journals. What should the article's title be? "FOX01 Mutations: A Common Link between Obesity and Alveolar Rhabdomyosarcoma"? He needed to come up with something punchier, more concise. "Obesity and Cancer: Genetic Correlations"? Maybe. He was confident that the publication would make a splash in Mexican newspapers, with dumbed-down headlines like "Mexican Doctor Discovers Cause of Cancer in Fat Gene," or "Love Handles and Tumors: The Secret Connection."

Emboldened by these high hopes, Aldama emailed the country's most renowned geneticist, inviting him to collaborate with him and Luis Ramírez: "We're almost certain that this sarcoma is related to the expression of a specific insulin-like growth factor," he wrote. He outlined his request that the researcher analyze the genome of various cell lines, signing off with a dramatic flourish: "This is by far the most fascinating case I have ever seen, and I think it merits a first-rate study by distinguished scientists such as yourself."

Aldama was well aware of the gossip that circulated in the institute's halls: that his enthusiasm was a product of Alzheimer's disease; that in the absence of a lover, he was seeking a Nobel Prize; that Dr. Quixote and his pathologist Sancho Panza were riding their feeble hypotheses through the uncharted realm of genomic science. He didn't care about the rumors. He believed that if envy were a virus, it would be herpes—common and opportunistic; fatal for the weak, but innocuous to the strong.

16

Paulina thought she was the only one in the family taking the news seriously that her father's cancer had spread. According to her mom, the doctor had been optimistic, but Paulina found that impossible to believe. All the websites she'd visited concurred that the prognosis for a metastatic sarcoma was very bleak. She wished she could go along to his appointments with her father, to confront the doctor with the questions her mother was unable to answer.

The anxiety, which felt so much like hunger, drove her to eat more compulsively than ever. She put on the pounds as quickly as her father lost them. Her friends tried to persuade her to trade cupcakes for carrots and chocolate for jicamas, but such light, nutritious snacks did little to relieve the stress overwhelming her.

The rest of Paulina's classmates, indifferent to her family strife, spared no time in making her the butt of their jokes, which until then had mostly been directed at her classmate Genaro, otherwise known as Porky the Brave.

The cure for her addiction came in the form of an accident at school. During a math class with the feckless Velociraptor—given this nickname for the way he flexed his arms with his head thrust forward—Paulina was gripped by a tremendous craving for carbs. That morning, she had neglected to restock her backpack with candy, and had nothing to tide her over until recess, when she could buy herself a *chilaquile* sandwich in the cafeteria. She daydreamed about the glorious medley of crusty bread, shredded and fried tortillas, salsa, chicken, and sour cream, glancing constantly at the clock as the Velociraptor jabbered on about obtuse angles in front of the blackboard.

She considered rounding out her lunch with a chocolate muffin and a spicy fruit lollipop. It seemed like a good idea to save half the muffin until school got out, so her hunger wouldn't torment her again on the long bus ride home, where Elodia would have prepared the afternoon meal.

Five minutes before the end of class, Paulina took out the exact change for the sandwich and muffin. She wanted to leave the classroom right away, to beat the lines in the cafeteria. Clutching the change in her left fist, she noted her homework down in her planner, and began putting her things away in her backpack.

When the bell rang, Paulina tried to spring to her feet, but due to an error in her calculation of her own girth, she got wedged in the gap between her desk and her chair, lost her balance, and fell to the floor with a crash. The chair landed on top of her, she got whacked on the head by her notebook, and her pencil case clattered onto the floor, scattering her pens and pencils beneath the desks.

"What's going on back there?" the Velociraptor asked, as a chorus of laughter celebrated the incident.

Paulina tried to get up, but her forty pounds of excess weight, the desk pinning her to the floor, and the fact that her free hand had been rendered useless by the change it was clutching, all made this impossible.

Genaro made a show of his alleged courage and rushed to Paulina's aid before her best friend Leonora could make her way over from across the room. They helped Paulina to her feet and picked up her scattered pencils and notebooks. Leonora stayed behind with her once the classroom had emptied.

"Did you hurt yourself badly?"

"No, just on the shoulder," Paulina said, nursing her injury.

"Do you want to go to the infirmary? I'll go with you."

"No, I'm fine."

"Let's go eat, I'll buy you whatever you want," Leonora suggested in an attempt to console her.

The clatter of her fall and her classmates' mocking laughter still reverberated deep inside Paulina. She tried to hold back the tears welling up in her eyes.

"I'm not hungry," she answered.

17

Elodia burst into the study, waking Ramón from an impromptu siesta.

"Señor! Help me with Benito, he's gotten out of his cage," she said in alarm.

Ramón leapt up with such haste that he felt dizzy and had to lean on his chair so as not to fall. He signaled to Elodia to help him walk. Linking arms like a pair of octogenarian sweethearts, they hurried outside. They found Benito perched on a branch in the ash tree overlooking the garden.

Would you look at that? thought Ramón, brimming with pride at Benito's feat. If I'd known you were so wily, I'd have named you after the cartel boss, what do they call him? El Chapo, Joaquín "el Chapo" Guzmán. Although you'd be "El Chapo" Martínez, obviously. You're family now.

"Come on, now, Benito, if you come down, I'll give you a treat!" shouted Elodia. "Want some tomato? Come down and get it."

Leave him alone, Ramón said inwardly. He'll come down soon.

The parrot looked delighted. He was perched on a thick, gnarled branch that was much more suitable for his claws than the flimsy canary perch where he spent his days. His lime-green feathers contrasted sharply with the ash tree's dark leaves.

Elodia was getting impatient. "I'll go fetch the garden hose, that'll teach him," she said under her breath with fascist determination.

Ramón intercepted her, urging her to calm down with a pontifical gesture.

Don't worry, Benito, I'll get this woman under control.

"You wouldn't believe the fright I got when I heard him cussing, and I turn around and what do I see? His cage is empty."

Ramón would have liked to know what Benito had squawked to celebrate his escape. At that moment the parrot was silent, studying them curiously.

"Shall I call the fire brigade?"

Don't talk such first-world nonsense, thought Ramón, shaking his head calmly from one side to the other. He pointed toward the kitchen and pretended to eat an egg-shaped vegetable.

"A tomato?"

Yes. Slice it up, thought Ramón, as he mimed his request.

Elodia followed his instructions precisely. She came back out with a plate of tomato chunks to offer Benito, lifting the plate up to the tree with both hands like an Aztec priest making an offering of a human heart to the gods.

Benito inspected the tomato curiously but didn't stir from his branch. Ramón approached Elodia, asked her to hand him the tomato, and urged her to leave him alone with the parrot. Once she had left the garden, Ramón went and sat down, and rested the plate on the table next to the open door of the cage.

I'm not going to pressure you. You clearly wanted out of that fucking cage. You figured out how it worked. You practiced. I salute you. You have every right to stay up there, but I'll tell you this, Benito. It won't be easy. There are lots of cats in the neighborhood. If you don't watch your ass, they could beat the crap out of you at any moment. They won't think twice about it, you'll have to be careful. And another thing: the cold. You have no idea how much the temperature drops out here. And you're from the jungle, you won't be able to handle it. I'm telling you now, so it won't be a nasty surprise. Think about it. Soon they'll bring me the money from the watch, and then I'll buy you that cage I promised you. Hell, do you want a girlfriend? I'll have them buy you one. The prettiest one around, nice and affectionate. What do you say? I'll have some cash in my pocket, you should take advantage. The clock's ticking. The other day I felt so beat up I went for my gun. I was about to pull the trigger, but I talked myself down. You have to wait for the right moment. That's why I'm telling you, if you come down here and hang on for a week at the most, then you'll see . . . a luxury pad, an old lady all to yourself. I'll understand if you turn down my offer. I sure as hell know what it's like to be shut in all day. And that's not all: the hunger, the nausea, the fucking pain, and the shaky legs. They keep telling me to be patient. But what for? I won't be able to do what I want. I'll just be a burden to my family. Me, I need to be in court. I need to be negotiating. When I was twenty, I worked for Villanueva in the Department of Labor. One day, he took me to lunch at the Bellinghausen, in the Zona Rosa. That was the first time I ever sat at a table with a white linen cloth and napkins. I felt like a king. Bring the young man a filet mignon, Villanueva told the waiter. It was exquisite. As soon as I could afford it, I went back to that same restaurant for a filet mignon. I ate there so many times, and I'll never be able to go back. Do you have any idea what it's like to live with the knowledge that you'll never eat another filet mignon at the Bellinghausen? There's no hope for me. But in your case, it's different: Check out this tomato. Doesn't it look tasty?

Despite the appetizing bait, Benito flitted from branch to branch until he reached the top of the tree, where he belted out a jubilant, "Son of a bitch!"

Ramón smiled with a mixture of pride and bitterness, envy and melancholy. Gazing up toward the sky where Benito was perched, he pictured the view of himself from those heights and felt dwarfed by the scene, far too small to spend so much money on doctors and medicines, too small for so much exhaustion and pain; he felt freed from the burden of being himself.

Then he imagined the landscape Benito could see: a forest of water towers, antennas, and high-rise buildings, wrapped in that dense cloud of dust and fumes they called smog—the name as ugly as what it described—which robbed the city of its most beautiful view: the volcanoes Popocatépetl and Iztaccíhuatl, the warrior with his smoking torch and the sleeping woman, the pair of lovers who sexed up the horizon. As a child, Ramón had often dreamed of climbing the volcanoes, touching the snow, peering into Popocatépetl's crater and catching a glimpse of the orange core of the earth. Ramón had lost the volcanoes just as he'd lost his innocence: without even noticing, many years before.

A gust of wind made the branches quiver, and soon there was a muffled thud in the bushes. Benito had fallen out of the tree. Ramón leapt up from his chair and hurried to pick him up in the front of his poncho. The parrot was so dazed that he didn't resist.

Back in his cage, Benito scarfed up the tomato; it had been several hours since he'd eaten a thing. To prevent another escape, Ramón secured the door with a wire knot. In less than a week, he promised the parrot, I'm going to get you a better cage.

18

"I don't feel like talking today," Teresa said, at the beginning of her session with her analyst.

"Why not?"

"I'm tired. But it's not just that. I was thinking on my way here that maybe two sessions a week is too much." She paused for a moment to reminisce. "I don't feel like I did back when I was seeing Ruffatto four days a week." Juan Luis Ruffatto was an Argentine psychoanalyst in exile, renowned for his vast erudition and the psychedelic retreats he ran in the new age mecca of Malinalco. "Back then, I really needed to talk and get it all out of my system, figure out what I'd done in the black hole between the divorce and my cancer. And the tough thing was realizing, after so much effort, that none of that talking had done any good."

"Well," her analyst interrupted, "I think that had a lot to do with Ruffatto and the fact that he wanted to sleep with you."

"Yes, but back then I really wanted an orthodox kind of analysis, and I ended up so shaken by the experience. When you suggested having two sessions a week, I wasn't sure, but then I thought, Okay, she's not just my therapist, she's my supervisor, too, and we have a lot to work on. And it's worked out. But now it's been, how long? Seven years?" Her analyst nodded. "I've grown a lot as a psychoanalyst, with your help, of course. I feel more confident with my patients every day, except for the few exceptions we've talked about. I feel like your supervision has helped me get over my insecurities as an analyst, but when it comes to my own therapy, I think . . . I don't know. I've been on the couch almost thirty years now. Even though I've more or less come to terms with myself and my decision to live alone, I'm still unsatisfied. At a certain point, doesn't it start to seem like a delusion?"

"The entire symbolic order can be seen as a delusion."

"Exactly," Teresa replied, "and sometimes I'd like to live more in the Imaginary, identify with my images of other people, get to know them and listen to them."

"Don't you get to know your patients? Don't you listen to them?"

"No, that's just what depresses me. I don't. Whenever I'm in a session, I spend the whole time trying to interpret the underlying messages, trying to connect what the patient says to what they've said before, or to what Freud wrote in such and such a book, or to whatever I happen to be studying at the time. What I mean is, I analyze my patients without listening to them. Obviously, I listen, but too actively. It's like I'm interrupting them the whole time in my head. And when I'm alone, the same thing happens. I can only be at peace with myself when I smoke pot, but the rest of the time I'm analyzing myself, and it obviously has to do with our sessions."

"How long have you felt this way?"

"I've been thinking . . . since I started seeing Ramón, the one who lost his tongue. It's amazing to see such a strong, vain, outgoing man suddenly reduced to nothing. His silence transformed him. I asked him if he feels like he has a phantom organ, but he just complains about the discomfort. It's typical for a patriarchal subject like him: life is all about working hard, being in control, feeling comfort or pleasure, or being angry. He doesn't understand what it means to be sick and in pain. Suddenly he doesn't know who he is. He's always having out-of-body experiences. He dreams about floating, touching the ceiling, looking down on his head and his sleeping body, and he's afraid that if he wakes up, he'll fall down and hit his head. He's detached from his body. I was thinking, that must be why monks take a vow of silence. The Buddhists, the Carthusians, the Trappists. Silence distances you from the flesh. Don't you think it's a paradox that something as invisible as speech should be precisely what keeps us tied to the body? The other day in therapy he started by writing about pollution, the air quality index, and the ozone layer. He's obsessed with the air quality in the city. He asks his daughter to check the government web page every day, to see how bad the smog's going to be. I think it's also a way of bonding with her. She's tried to teach him to use the Internet, but he's not interested. It's like he associates technology with his mortality, with his own planned obsolescence."

"How do you connect that obsession to what you're going through?" the analyst asked.

"Well, I think his silence, the tracheotomy, and now the

metastasis they found on his lung all have something to do with it. The bad news about his lung doesn't seem to have affected him on a conscious level. Maybe he's repressing it, or displacing it onto the issue of his estate, but the other possibility is that he no longer identifies with his body, and that's why it doesn't matter to him. He hasn't shown any emotional response."

"Do you identify with that?"

"What?" asked Teresa.

"His relationship to his body."

"I don't think so. I don't know. I probably identify with him because, since he can't speak, I talk much more than I usually would, and I've told him personal stories about my treatment and what the chemo was like—losing my hair, the hot flashes, and everything else. At the same time, I've realized he doesn't identify with me as a patient, even though his chemo has been horrific. It's almost as if he doesn't identify those things as happening to him, even though he's obviously in pain. He's really suffering a lot."

"You identify with him, but he doesn't with you . . ."

"I guess I identify with him because we're both patients in his session, and because I've tried to achieve the same detachment he feels from his cancer. He has no interest in the disease, it doesn't speak to him. He sees it as an accident, like having the flu, and in that sense he has a healthy attitude. Just think how much worse it would be for him if he were torturing himself with the question of what he's done wrong, which emotions he's repressing, and everything else. I think the loss of his tongue, along with the fact that he's not a spiritual person, saved him from that identification between mind and body that can be so harmful, and which did me so much damage, despite the fact that my cancer was hereditary, and I was already high-risk. Even though I knew all that, I felt like it was my fault, that something was wrong with me. He doesn't feel that way. His amputation spared him from all those narcissistic fictions that identify the self with the body. For me, it was the opposite: when they took away my breasts, I suffered a total loss of self. It's been so many years, and I still don't . . ."

Teresa fell silent, assuming that her analyst would end the session there. She was wrong.

"You describe him as wise and enlightened, but he also sounds like he's full of fear. There's something that doesn't add up. Is it possible that his silence has somehow seduced you, and prevented you from being disappointed by what he might otherwise be saying? When someone's quiet, they seem not to possess that excessive jouissance that torments us, that total otherness that prevents identification. And that's why, as Lacanians, we aren't supposed to speak during our sessions. But now I think we should explore your eagerness to leave analysis from both perspectives. It seems like having to talk more in your sessions with this patient is leading you to believe in the promise of desire again. His silence means you don't have to face the void at its core."

"*This* is exactly what I think isn't working." Teresa emphasized the neutral pronoun to make the object of her dismissal more ambiguous. "Psychoanalysis is based on the supposed need to put the unconscious into words, to neutralize the metonymies of impossible desire. But what I'm seeing is that you can take a shortcut to hold on to the void, and cut off the need for small talk with a single stroke. We know talking alone won't save us from the Real."

Teresa had gained the upper hand by challenging the validity of the theory that upheld their trade. Her analyst's response was openly defensive.

"Then why keep seeing him, if he doesn't need psycho-analysis? Don't you think you could be sabotaging his treatment, as you have with other patients?"

She was alluding to the neurotic aversion to men that Teresa had developed after her mastectomy. According to her discoveries in analysis, this hatred was a defense mechanism: to preempt the possibility of a man spurning her incomplete body, she had banished men from her libidinal spectrum. But Teresa resisted this interpretation, instead favoring a classic Freudian reading: once the possibility of motherhood was lost to her, men, mere accessories of the penis, had lost their value. Unfortunately, her maternal feelings toward Eduardo didn't fit neatly into this theory. Still, Teresa had never fully accepted that her difficulties with her male patients were the result of a psychological defense mechanism. There was another possibility, the simplest one: that men were more challenging patients due to their macho defenses against sharing their feelings with a woman. Not only could men not cry, they couldn't accept that a woman should occupy a position of authority over them, not even in the intimacy of the psychoanalyst's office.

"My experience with Ramón is completely different from those I had with my patients back then. It's not that he's a macho and can't express his feelings. I mean, certainly he's a macho, that goes without saying, but his feelings are very raw, and they have less to do with the threat of his cancer than with a serious moral dilemma, and his grief for the person he used to be. And I keep seeing him because, although he may seem enlightened," Teresa added reproachfully, "he does have a serious conflict, not with his cancer, but with the death drive itself. When someone loses the objects of his libido—in his case, language and professional success—the death drive can turn against the ego, and that's exactly what I think's happening in his case. He's feeling at peace because he's planning to kill himself as soon as he decides it's time. I want to prevent that from happening. I'm not seeing him just for fun."

To ease the hostility that had arisen between them, the analyst changed the subject.

"How have you handled the marijuana issue with him?"

Teresa accepted the truce.

"I suggested it gently and he didn't want to hear anything about it. Partly because of the usual prejudices, and partly because he sublimates all of his physical discomfort, all the neuralgias, the bleeding, everything, into the fact that he doesn't want to pay back his debt to his brother. He thinks of his own suffering as a kind of atonement that frees him from the moral obligation to pay up. If he hasn't committed suicide yet, it's only because he hasn't met the quota of physical suffering that would let him rest easy over something that, deep down, he thinks is a scam. That's why he's accepting the pain. Thank God he doesn't have the money to pay his brother, otherwise he'd already have killed himself."

"And how does marijuana come in to all this?"

"The cancer has spread to his lung, and some marijuana could really help him, as much to relieve the pain as to eliminate the cells . . . I know you think I'm deluded, but it really works. I'm not crazy."

"If I thought you were crazy, I'd be betraying everything I believe about the human mind," the analyst answered in a friendly tone.

"I know. Pay no attention to me. It's just that it infuriates me to be surrounded by so much hypocrisy."

"Which proves you're not crazy," the analyst joked. "We've gotten sidetracked from an important issue. You were thinking about only coming once a week. Would you also stop seeing new patients? It seems like you're quite overbooked."

"My superego won't let me. It's tough for patients to find a therapist who understands them like I do, who can relate to their experience."

"You could invite them to the support groups you run, and maybe give up your Saturday sessions."

Teresa thought immediately of Eduardo, whose mother could only bring him to therapy on weekends. Teresa didn't want to abandon him, even though it might be a good idea for her to pass him on to an analyst like Ruffatto, a man with an air of distinction whom Eduardo could see as an authority figure.

"I don't know," she said after a long silence. "I'd rather take a vacation. It's been years since I've gone anywhere. But who would water my plants? Seriously, they need more care than a husband." The analyst forced a smile to acknowledge the joke. "What I really need," Teresa went on, "is a vacation from myself, from myself as an analyst and a patient, coordinator, gardener, everything. I'd like to go to the beach and just sleep for a while."

The analyst remained silent. Teresa resorted to an existentialist cliché.

"Sartre says that hell is other people, and he's right. The problem is that sometimes I'm somebody else, and that makes me my own personal hell, all to myself."

Again, the analyst didn't answer.

"Now I feel like you're not ending the session because I said I didn't want to come twice a week anymore. The question, of course, is whether I no longer *should* come twice a week," Teresa said lightly.

Teresa was determined to put her analyst in the mythical "place of truth" regarding the question of the frequency of her sessions. All analysts must refuse to adopt that symbolic role: the truth lies not in them, but in the analysand's unconscious. So the analyst shifted the focus to one of Teresa's verbal tics.

"You've said the word 'obviously' several times today. What do you think it means?"

"That's obvious," Teresa said with a wry smile.

Nothing could be obvious for a psychoanalyst, but she needed someone for whom it was, someone who didn't analyze her every word, who didn't question every single thing she said, but accepted it as a transparent window into her soul. Teresa also wanted to listen to someone, not out of professional duty, but out of affection and curiosity. It wasn't the excess of analysis that wearied her, but the absence of its opposite—words that were friendly and honest, spoken for their own sake.

"When shall we meet again?" the analyst asked.

"Tuesday, as usual."

19

Carmela arrived home after two hours in heavy traffic. It was already late. She found Paulina in the kitchen doing her homework and scolded her for not being in bed. She ate a bowl of cereal for dinner, washed the dish slowly, and climbed the stairs at the pace of an exhausted mountaineer. When she reached the top, she rested one side of her head against Mateo's door, to hear if he was still awake. She found Ramón in the bedroom watching the news, asked how he was feeling, told him to turn off the TV, removed the gold watch from her purse, and placed it undramatically on the bed.

"Why didn't you tell me?"

Ramón stared at the watch as if it were a used condom found between his daughter's sheets. He demanded an explanation.

"I asked Leonardo why he came to see you the other day. The poor guy's a terrible liar. He's never going to make it as a lawyer." She sat down on the bed, resting a hand on her husband's left foot. "Why did you want to sell it? That's not going to solve anything."

Ramón picked up his notebook, opened it to a new page, and wrote: *You shouldn't be meddling in my affairs.*

"I don't have any choice, do I? I'm not going to sell off my jewelry until the day we have nothing to eat. Until then, I'd rather know it's still there"—she gestured toward the closet—"and could help us get out of a tight spot. And you still haven't told me why you wanted the money."

For the notary fee and the deed. I'm signing the house over to you before the other thing.

"Are you still going on about that? I'm not divorcing you even if you cheat on me with Elodia, okay? And why do you need to sign the house over to me? You have a will. And anyway, nothing's going to happen!"

Ramón urged her to give back his notebook.

In case I'm not around anymore, I don't want to leave you in a bind. You have no idea what Ernesto's capable of.

"We'll pay him back in installments. You're not signing your half of the house over to me, and we're not getting divorced, okay? You're going to finish your chemo and keep getting better. You just have to make up your mind: I'm going to beat this. And one day you'll be able to leave that watch to your son."

Slob'll just sell it. He's such a dumbass.

"And we'll tell him all about the day we bought it, and how happy we were. Remember?"

Ramón nodded.

"Then don't go selling off our memories. And certainly not behind my back. I have enough on my plate with everyone out there treating me like a moron. 'Poor thing,' the boss's wife who can't handle a lawsuit. Everyone's against me, even your secretary, who by the way is a fucking misogynist." Ramón was taken aback to hear her swear. "That's right. I can't stand that bitch, but since I don't have the luxury of being able to pay her off, I have to put up with her. And then Leonardo shows up with his tail between his legs, and I have to force him to confess."

I'll send him a message: Thanks for your loyalty, you pussy.

"How do you expect me to feel? Put yourself in my shoes."

Ramón seemed genuinely remorseful. He tried to make peace with a joke.

Don't be mad. I get it. I'll put myself in your shoes. Hell, I'll even put myself in your high heels, but we've got to go to the courthouse. It's for our own good.

"We're not going, and you'd better not put my heels on. Remember what happened the day I did your makeup."

Elodia crossed herself with unusual fervor as she ventured out of the Martínezes' house with a gold watch hidden between her breasts. Ramón had convinced her to help him out by telling her that with part of the money from the sale of the watch, he would pay her overdue wages and buy Benito a respectable cage.

Elodia's mission was to go downtown by public transport—Ramón didn't have enough cash to send her by taxi—and get back before the children arrived home from school.

She hurried toward the bus stop, the cold metal rubbing against the warm skin beneath her bra. The gold filled her with paranoia. Everyone was staring at her, everyone knew there was a dazzling solid gold treasure tucked inside her blouse. When she tried to pay the bus driver, she dropped the coins. She crouched down to pick them up, taking care not to lean forward so the watch wouldn't slither out of its hiding place. She sat down by the window and pretended to drift off to sleep, disguising her nerves about the thieves she imagined were lying in wait.

She arrived safe and sound at the metro station and crept gingerly down the steps, fearing an accident that might imperil the integrity of the watch. She felt anxious and unprotected, but also prettier, younger, and whiter, as if the gold in her bosom brought her closer to the ideal of beauty imposed and coveted by the conquistadors. Gold was the adornment of choice for kings, bishops, and cartel bosses; it was a material of extremes, beloved as much by God as by Satan.

She got off the metro at the Zócalo. *Watch out for pickpockets in the city center*, Ramón had warned her. She stepped out into the street in front of the cathedral, quaking with fear. She crossed herself again, took out the directions Ramón had given her to the jewelry store, studied the map, and set out decisively in the wrong direction. At the corner of Correo Mayor and República de Guatemala, she realized she was lost. She saw a gang of drug addicts coming toward her. They were probably devotees of the skeletal Santa Muerte. A shiver ran down her spine. If I run, she thought, they'll catch up with me. She froze in terror. She felt as if the gold were crying out, "Here I am!" from between her breasts. She was afraid her pounding heart would dislodge the watch from its place. She stood rigidly to attention and waited for the miscreants to pass by. They didn't turn back to look at her.

She wandered for two more blocks trying to find her bearings and asked for directions from a street vendor, who sent her back to the Zócalo down a dismal side street, where a roving popsicle salesman almost frightened her to death. Back at the main square, she spotted a fair-haired man who looked very friendly, and asked him for help.

"Excuse me," she said to the fellow, who turned out to be a Dutch tourist. "Which way is Madero?"

Despite his broken Spanish, he managed to point her in the right direction, thanks to his trusty compass and an enormous map of the city center.

She arrived at the jeweler's in one piece and asked to speak to the manager. She explained that she'd come on behalf of Señor Martínez and gave him a card where Ramón described in detail the history of his relationship with the owners of Tepeyac Jewelry and expressed his desire to sell them the watch.

"I've hidden it," Elodia whispered. "Can I use your bathroom?"

Once she was alone in the tiny cubicle, Elodia sat down on the toilet, unbuttoned her blouse, and removed the watch, which she'd wrapped in a grocery bag to prevent it from getting soaked in sweat.

The jeweler asked her to wait at the counter while he tested the gold's purity.

"Where are you going?" she asked suspiciously.

"To appraise the watch."

Ramón hadn't warned her that this would happen.

"Can't you do it here?"

"No, ma'am, but don't worry. I'll be right back."

Elodia wondered what she would do if the manager didn't come back soon, or if he came out playing dumb, as if he'd never seen her before. What if they swindled her? Her employer had seemed desperate when he'd begged her to do him this favor, and had sworn her to secrecy, since he was going to use part of the money for a "surprise" for Señora Martínez. Elodia had thought that the story sounded odd, but she accepted it out of respect for her boss, and because she urgently needed the overdue paychecks he'd promised her. But who were the police more likely to believe? The manager of a prestigious jewelry store, or a domestic worker who didn't even have a voter ID? She wouldn't just lose her job, they would also send her to jail, to the Santa Martha Acatitla penitentiary, where she'd be locked away with murderesses and kidnappers and skin-headed gang members covered in tattoos, who would demand money from her children in exchange for not beating her up.

"How about fifty thousand?" the manager asked when he came back to the counter.

Elodia shuddered when he named the price. She'd known they would pay her a lot, but not that much. How was she going to hide such a huge amount in her bra? She tried to disguise her mortification and took out her cell phone to call Señor Martínez. Ramón picked up the phone and tinkled a bell to let her know he was listening.

She spoke in a piercing voice, as if he were half deaf as well as mute.

"I'm here with the gentleman at the store!" She lowered her voice from a shout to a whisper. "He says it'll be fifty thousand."

Ramón had told her that he would tap the table once to indicate that he rejected the offer, and twice to accept. Elodia had memorized this simple code by repeating, "One tap no, two taps yes," to herself over and over.

Ramón gave two firm taps on the table.

"So, yes?"

She heard two taps again.

"Okay. So I'll take a taxi this time?"

Two taps. Elodia said goodbye, and Ramón hung up.

On her way back, Elodia fantasized about all the things she could have bought with the money she was carrying: a washing machine, a gas stove and oven, a nice pair of shoes, a new computer for her children, a water heater for her shower, and an endless array of hair accessories, her only weakness.

Mesmerized by her consumerist daydreams, Elodia forgot to tell the driver to take a left turn. They had to take a long detour before reaching the house. As they drove, she recalled the passage in the Gospels where Jesus proclaimed that no man could serve two masters, God and money.

"I'm back!" Elodia announced in triumph as she entered the house.

Ramón was awaiting her anxiously. It was an anticlimactic encounter, since rather than handing over the money immediately, Elodia had to go up to the bathroom to extricate the wad of bills from between her breasts.

When he finally had the bills in his grip, still warm from their prolonged contact with Elodia's skin, Ramón counted them eagerly. It had been a long time since he'd held such undiluted power in his hands. The faces of dozens of Sor Juanas and General Zaragozas gazed at him solemnly from the paper notes, indifferent to the earthly delight that lit up their owner's face. With them, Ramón would be able to speak again; with them, he would grandiloquently dictate his final wish.

20

Aldama read the offensive reply from the director of the UNAM Biomedical Research Institute several times. It began with an unforgivably careless mistake, addressing him as "Dear Doctor Madame." The implied emasculation might have enraged an insecure man, but Aldama was annoyed that his correspondent hadn't bothered to proofread his message before sending it, and correct the mindlessly cyber-generated autocorrect. The famous geneticist went on to excuse his delayed response with a joke about his work on tissue regeneration: "My apologies for not writing sooner, but sometimes we have to choose between opening axolotls and emails." Aldama might have taken delight in this witticism, but under the circumstances he saw it as shameless proof of just how insignificant his interlocutor thought him.

With no further diplomatic preamble, the genetic researcher informed him that the institute's interest in cancer cells was limited to the study of telomeres, the caps found at each end of a chromosome, the front and back covers of the genetic book, designed to protect its hereditary inner pages during cell division. Just as handling and friction with other surfaces caused the covers of books to deteriorate, the jostling caused by meiosis eroded the telomeres, speeding up the cellular aging process. Sometimes, carcinogenesis involved the reactivation of the telomerase enzyme, which could repair the telomeres after each division. In this way, the cancer cells avoided natural wear and tear and remained eternally young.

The geneticist's detailed description of telomeres showed how little faith he had in the physiological knowledge of a clinical oncologist like Aldama and represented a worse affront than the previous ones. But what most incensed Aldama on reading the missive was the discovery that Luis Ramírez, the pathologist who'd encouraged him to pursue the study in the first place, had been using him only to further his personal goals: "Dr. Ramírez has expressed his interest in participating in our telomere study at his own laboratory using your patient's cell line, as well as some others they're working with. We're sure this collaboration will benefit his Institute as much as ours." That scumbag Ramírez had "expressed his interest." He'd never cared about the rhabdomyosarcoma's oncogenes; what he was really after was a cell line that secreted telomerase, just as Ramón's rhabdomyoblasts did. Everything else, Aldama's participation included, was incidental. The geneticist signed off with a categorical statement: "It would be impossible to demonstrate even a correlation between the FOXO1 alleles linked to hereditary obesity and the oncogenesis of such an unusual tumor. Frankly, I think your working hypothesis is unsound."

Not only did he feel duped by Ramírez, but after the tactless researcher's ridicule, Aldama was embarrassed by his naïve scientific ideas. In the end, the gossips were right: his foray into genomics was a senile folly. He cursed his own arrogance: doctors should be content to stick to their Hippocratic mission, charging handsome fees while they plied their trade. The parallel joys of saving lives and making a fortune were enough to satisfy most oncologists, but not Aldama. He recalled a passage from Saint Augustine that captured his feelings for scientific research: "Late have I loved you, beauty so ancient and so new, late have I loved you." Late had he loved microscopes and spectrometers. Late had he loved the elegant double helix of DNA. Late had he known the thrill of hunting down founder mutations that explained de profundis the causes of life, not just of its oncological quirks, but of evolution itself through the ages, from the remotest primordial soup to the cunning biped who looks in the mirror and believes himself superior to his own nature.

Aldama accepted stoically that he would never discover the cause of Ramón Martínez's cancer, a dauntless strain of muscular cells that had eluded eight cycles of aggressive chemotherapy and two months of radiation.

The rhabdomyoblasts had also had the last laugh, coating the patient's lungs with moss and the reef of his spine with coral. Where else might they now be dwelling? When he gave Ramón the news that he couldn't be cured, that the disease was continuing to progress, he had seemed relieved, as if the treatment had convinced him that, in his case, the happiest diagnosis was a terminal one. Mrs. Martínez, on the other hand, had responded with irate questions that did more to accuse him of incompetence than request information. How was it possible that after such harsh and lengthy treatment, the doctor did nothing but show them the whitish areas on the chest X-rays where the cancer was thriving? Aldama tried to explain that without chemotherapy, her husband probably wouldn't have survived even two months. Despite the unusually aggressive sarcoma, the patient was still alive almost a year after his diagnosis. Under the circumstances, the treatment had been quite successful. Mrs. Martínez then asked defiantly how the study with the original tumor's cells was progressing. It was all a ploy, Aldama would have liked to tell her, to use your husband's tissue in a cellular aging project. The search for the fountain of eternal genetic youth will bear fruit many years from now, when it's no longer of use to your husband or me, since I'm about to retire and be consigned to oblivion. I've treated hundreds of patients and cured many of them, but I can count those who remember me with gratitude on just one hand.

He answered that the cellular research had been effective for designing the chemotherapy, thanks to which, he reiterated, the patient's survival had been extended by almost a year. Mrs. Martínez asked no further questions and began to cry with restraint. The patient consoled her fondly. Aldama took the chance to observe her. He had dealt with dozens of relatives and knew how to judge their character. Throughout the treatment, Mrs. Martínez had been calm and collected. Many patients' husbands and wives were dramatic, obstreperous, demanding. Despite the circumstances, they wanted to be the center of attention. Not her. She had accompanied her husband discreetly to dozens of appointments, waited for hours outside the chemotherapy suite, stood in interminable lines to donate blood, collect lab results, and deliver urine samples. She had never shown any sign of clinging to religion or even to optimism, that secular superstition. She had carried herself in a way he could only describe as the epitome of civilization. He understood her anger: she had done everything she could, and the doctor had let her down. Nevertheless, it wasn't his job to apologize like a hotel manager to an unsatisfied guest. Medicine was a rudimentary and to a large extent intuitive trade, from which it was impossible to expect perfect results.

Many believed that, in the end, scientific progress would conquer cancer, and oncology would become as crude a specialty as orthodontics. Patients would seek treatment for a brain tumor as nonchalantly as they made an appointment to have a tooth pulled. But Aldama didn't believe the civilized world would prosper long enough for that oncological paradise to become a reality.

21

"Asshoooooole! Asshoooooole!" Benito began to squawk when he sensed that Ramón was about to get home. Elodia, the only witness to the parrot's daily prophecies, always recounted them to Ramón, and today was no exception.

"I was upstairs cleaning when I heard Benito squawking. That'll be Señor Martínez, I said, so I came straight down to pour you a glass of *horchata*. I figured you'd be thirsty in this heat."

I appreciate it, thought Ramón, and he went out to visit Benito, who celebrated his arrival with even more obscene squawks. Benito's new cage was the avian equivalent of a Hollywood mansion: twelve cubic feet, six mahogany perches at multiple different heights, a metal ladder that led to a balcony, a swing, a pool with an island and a miniature plastic palm tree, an automatic food dispenser, insulating night cover, and a slide-out tray for easy cleaning. A pair of macaws could have lived comfortably in those luxury quarters, which took up most of the space on the garden table.

Aren't you embarrassed, Ramón asked Benito, to know you don't live like President Juárez anymore, but like fucking Maximilian? Oh yeah, he was a great humanist and all that crap. Why did he go around being so meddlesome? The word "meddlesome" was one of a number of linguistic relics making their way into Ramón's mute soliloquies. These archaisms that came from his mother's vocabulary had never featured in Ramón's speech before, but the thick current of his silence had stirred the bed of his memory, dredging up old-fashioned words like "bungling," "trinkets," "baubles," "harlot," "victuals," and "valise." According to Teresa, these terms' resurgence was a sign that his mind had undertaken a review of his past, in search of records that might account for the present. Our strongest desire in life, his therapist had said, is to understand why.

They took the catheter out of my chest today, Ramón told his friend. They're taking me off the chemo, so I don't need it anymore. The palliative care doctor wanted to leave it in and use it for painkillers, but I told them it was itchy and asked them to take it out. I don't want to die with a tube in my chest, it gives me the creeps. But the pain in my legs is really a bitch. The tumor's pressing on the nerves in my spine, so I've got sciatica all over the place. They'll give me some hot compresses for the inflammation, but just now in the car it hurt like hell, you have no idea. Every time we went over a speed bump, I felt like my balls were being crushed. Sometimes I wonder what they did about tumors in ancient times. Turns out cancer existed thousands of years ago. Paulina and I looked it up on the Internets. Even the dinosaurs had to deal with this motherfucker. And these days, sea lions are getting cancer of the nuts from polluted water. I can't remember where, but somewhere in the U.S. And you know what country has more cancer than anywhere else? Tere says it's Canada, because of all the preservatives. She thinks anything natural's good for you, even scorpion venom. And then there's the weed. I have to admit, it feels good. And then the doctor gives me these opiate concoctions, which at the end of the day are the same shit the Chinese used to smoke, except these are prescription and cost an arm and a leg. What the fuck's up with that? Tere told me she gets her marijuana for free, someone gives it to her for helping out. But who? What for? There's something sketchy about it. Remember this: there's no such thing as a free lunch. But she talked it up so much I finally gave in. She took out a little gadget that looked like a radio, except it had a straw where the antenna would be, and told me to take a drag on it, like a cigarette. It's not smoke, she said, it's a vaporizer. Nothing happened. She told me to take another hit, so I did. You won't believe this: five minutes later, I had a hard-on. I'd almost forgotten what it felt like to have a boner. It was so weird, my back was hurting like a motherfucker, but then it stopped. No pain at all. I was pretty high by then—my face was tingling, and everything was moving in slow motion. And I started feeling horny, I swear. Not because of the doctor, poor old lady, just in general. And the pain was gone. How are you feeling? she asked me. I just gave her the thumbs-up—I'm doing great. If you'd told me twenty years ago I'd be doing drugs, I'd have said no way, you're out of your mind. But now look at me. She asked me something or other, I can't remember what. So, I looked at the keyboard to answer, and I'll be damned if the keys weren't talking. It was the weirdest thing. I stared at them and completely spaced out. I could hear them all: *aaaa, teee, rrrr, uuuu*. When I came down, I was lying comfortably on the couch. She brought me a glass of milk and said, Here, have a drink of this. Carmela was waiting for me outside, and Tere had told her I wasn't feeling well and had taken a little nap. I went out with a serious face and she didn't suspect a thing. Tere said if I want, she could give me some to use at home. Can you imagine us doing drugs here, Benito? There's no chance in hell I'm letting my kids catch me smoking pot. What kind of example am I setting if their last memory of their father is seeing him stoned? No way. But I'll ask her for some when I go to her place next week . . . It could be the last. I already transferred the ownership of the house, now we just need to get the divorce papers done. Once Carmela accepted that my number's up, she stopped arguing. The other day, she asked if I wanted her to call Ernesto and tell him. No way, I said, over my dead body. I don't want that asshole to find out until after I'm gone. He can come to the funeral and cry for his money. Carmela didn't make a stink about it, so I took the chance to bring up the divorce. She doesn't want to do it, she's ashamed of what people will think. Who? I asked her. She says there'll be a record on paper. True, marital status is recorded on the death certificate. But who cares? Who's going to find out? The children! she said. We can explain it, I said, we have nothing to hide. She still doesn't want to. Mateo's about to fail the whole school year, and Pau's depressed and refusing to eat. Take her to therapy. With what money? I bet Tere would help us out for free. You can count on her. We'll ask her to help us explain the divorce. Stop going on about that! she shouted. But I want to go without any worries, I wrote. And what about me? she asked. I have to stay! If I could speak, I wouldn't have known what to say . . . I get where she's coming from, Benito, but if Ernesto buys himself a judge and gets a writ of seizure, he could really fuck them over. It's not like he earned that money he lent me by honest means. He did it by shafting his suppliers and employees. And I defended him and his dirty tricks. He's a thug, a gangster. And I'm hardly a socialist, but someone's got to make sure a predator like that is the one who gets fucked.

Benito swung vigorously on his swing and seemed to approve of Ramón's plans, nodding his head in agreement again and again.

22

Aldama's cell phone rang at eleven on Monday night. He had withdrawn to his study after dinner to listen to music. The two glasses of wine he'd drunk put him in the mood to search through his CDs for Aram Khachaturian's expansive *Masquerade Suite*. At least the termination of his genetic research had given him back those precious evening hours he spent indulging his fanatical devotion to music, the only time he could call *free* in every sense of the word.

"Forgive me for calling at this hour," Mrs. Martínez said, "but I had to stay late at the office today, and when I got home, I found my husband in a terrible state, collapsed on the floor next to our bed."

Aldama harbored profound nostalgia for the pager, that little gadget, a relic from the last century that had received electronic messages before the widespread use of cell phones. If anyone wanted to speak to him, they had to call an operator, who would transcribe the message, request a name and phone number, and send it to his pager: "Doctor, the bleeding started again. What should we do?" "Vomiting and diarrhea, not sure if urgent." "The hospital called. Mrs. Ibáñez died. Sincerely, Sara." Never had patients and relatives been so plainspoken and succinct as in the glorious heyday of the pager.

"Tell me, what happened?"

"He stood up to go to the bathroom and couldn't even manage three steps. He had a terrible cramp, and didn't make it in time . . . I had to change his clothes, and then I woke up my son to help me lift him onto the bed. I've given him a tramadol, but it hasn't helped."

"You gave him one capsule?"

"That's right. And he'd already had one this afternoon, apart from the ketorolac."

"Okay. Give him another tramadol right away, and ask the pharmacy to deliver some Celebrex, two hundred milligrams. When the Celebrex arrives, give him one of those and a Dormicum. That should get him to sleep."

"What was the name of the pills again?"

"Ce-le-brex, with an x. Come by my office tomorrow morning after ten and tell my secretary you need a prescription for some transdermal patches. She'll give you some instructions on how to use them."

"Thank you so much. I'll be there tomorrow."

"Perfect. And tell your husband not to worry. Those patches work miracles."

They said goodbye.

Aldama thought of how the patient's nerves would be calmed once they'd been pumped full of opiates. They would no longer bombard his consciousness with constant updates on the ruinous state of the nation. Because, after all, pain was essentially knowledge. That was why flagellants whipped themselves: so great was their emptiness, so ignorant were they, that even the knowledge of that pain gave them pleasure. And that, too, was the very reason so many people were hooked on heroin: so great was the adversity in which they lived that their only form of knowledge was through pain, pain which they sought to numb with the needle. Your husband, he would have liked to tell Mrs. Martínez, knows all too well what's happening to him, that's precisely why he's suffering, and why he cries out in pain. Have you ever seen *Collective Suicide*, the painting by Siqueiros at the Museum of Modern Art in New York? I recommend it highly; it captures what's going on inside your husband at this very moment.

He poured himself a glass of whiskey in silence. It was too late to still be thinking about the clinic or go back to listening to the impassioned Khachaturian. He needed to relax, and what better way to do so than with Johann Sebastian Bach's Cantata BWV 82, sung by Lorraine Hunt, the mezzo-soprano? She'd died of hereditary breast cancer in 2006. Her husband, the composer Peter Lieberson, of lymphoma in 2011.

Aldama had a particular interest in music associated with cancer. He'd devoted a great deal of time to listening to the complete works of Brahms, who had probably died of cancer of the liver or pancreas. When he learned that the conductor Claudio Abbado had died of stomach cancer, he obtained all his CDs and set about searching for contrasts between the recordings before and after his illness. He had also ordered an unfamiliar album from London: Iannis Xenakis's *Metastasis*, which turned out to be a pile of "stochastic" garbage.

He removed the Khachaturian CD from the stereo and replaced it with the cantatas performed by Hunt. Though her voice was generally too operatic for Bach's compositions, the singer convincingly embodied the psychic drama of Simeon, the biblical character invoked in the cantata. Perhaps cancer, which by the time she recorded that album had already done away with her mother and sister, had granted the mezzo-soprano a maturity perfectly suited to that work based on an unusually poignant episode from the Gospels. Joseph and Mary took the baby Jesus to present him at the temple, where the elderly Simeon recognized him as his Savior, and, holding him in his arms, sang, "It is enough": *Ich habe genug*. It was a familiar mixture to Aldama: surfeit and plenitude.

"*Ich habe den Heiland, das Hoffen der Frommen, Auf meine begierigen Arme genommen.*" I have held the Savior, the hope of the righteous, in the warm embrace of my arms.

"*Ich habe genug.*"

As Lorraine Hunt's voice softened the harsh German syllables, Aldama hummed the beautiful melody.

"*Nun wünsch ich, noch heute mit Freuden Von hinnen zu scheiden.*" Now I wish to depart from here with joy this very day.

Simeon was old and weary. The child's delicate freshness intensified the weight of his years. He sang as if saying, "Jesus, I leave the world in your hands. Now is my time to sleep."

"*Ich habe genug.*"

Aldama savored the end of the aria with a swig of whiskey. Silence. The composition continued with a fervent recitative.

"*Ach! möchte mich von meines Leibes Ketten Der Herr erretten!*" Ah! If only the Lord would free me from the enslavement of my body.

The cantata was also a crash course in preparation for death. Another pause. Another swig of whiskey. The composition arrived at its final aria.

"*Ich freue mich auf meinen Tod . . .*" With gladness, I look forward to my death. Ah! If only it had already come. Then I should escape the despair that keeps me captive now on earth.

Only a fanatical Lutheran could have written such a joyful celebration of death. What better way to indoctrinate a terminal patient than with such compelling music? Aldama wanted that cantata, in that same version, to accompany him at his final hour.

When Simeon sang, holding Jesus in his arms, the child was unaware of the future awaiting him on the cross. Had he had any idea, he would have howled in fright. Aldama remembered from the catechism that Jesus had at least been aware of his fate the night before his capture, in the Garden of Gethsemane. Why hadn't he hightailed it to Galilee, as so many rebels later did? The passion of Christ, with so many excruciating stages, was a kind of postgraduate degree in anatomy. In the end, Christ became such an expert that he managed to solve the riddle of death. So much pain, so much knowledge: thus was he able to rise on the third day from the tomb, well rested, and disappear. Why hadn't he stayed behind, in body and soul, to fight for eternal life on earth? Perhaps in the throes of pain he had foreseen that it was a lost cause, that no one else would be willing to suffer— to learn—as much as it would take to cease to be a man and to become a god.

"It is enough," Jesus must have thought in Aramaic, before vanishing into the ether.

"We regret to inform you that humans have metastasized into the Congo, Siberia, Borneo, and the Amazon."

Who would be the world's oncologist? Aldama wondered before turning out the light and heading to bed.

"*Ich habe genug.*"

23

After two weeks without seeing Ramón, Teresa received a message from him. "I'm still having trouble with my legs. Good evening. Do you think what we talked about would help with the inflammation? R.M., Esq." She replied straightaway that it would, and that she'd be happy to deliver the "medicine" the next day. Teresa was accustomed to using euphemisms for marijuana, since almost none of her patients felt comfortable with that word so fraught with myths, stigma, and class prejudice. She favored the scientific name, *Cannabis sativa*, which she found feminine and suggestive. She associated "*sativa*" with satisfaction and *sapientia*—Latin for wisdom— which seemed to her like kindred states of mind.

Ramón was in no state to be able to smoke a joint or get hold of a vaporizer, so she decided to make him some cannabutter cookies that he could soften with milk and eat discreetly, since he didn't want to tell his family about the new treatment. To begin, she placed a stick of butter and two tablespoons of finely ground bud in a frying pan. Once the butter had melted, she stirred the ingredients together, simmering them slowly until the liquid had turned a bright pistachio-green. In a glass bowl, she beat two egg yolks, one egg white, one and a half cups of flour, and a spoonful of baking powder. Then she added half a cup of sugar, and another of cocoa powder, whose only purpose was to disguise the dough's suspicious color. Finally, she added the *sativa* butter. When the dough was ready, she shaped it into fifteen cookies, arranged them on a baking sheet, and put them in the oven, preheated to 325 degrees. For fifteen minutes, the heat caressed them, made them rise, crisped them, and turned their edges a golden brown. They looked so good that she couldn't resist having one herself. She sat down with a book of surrealist paintings to enjoy the cookie's visual effects. After a while of leafing through the pages, she masturbated then and there. She climaxed with a frenzied tapestry beneath her eyelids: mangoes, lemons, and peaches everywhere.

The next morning, she woke up slightly hungover. She had trouble getting through her morning sessions. After lunch, revived by an espresso, she set out in the direction of Ramón's house.

The domestic worker greeted her with suspicion, as if Teresa were a health inspector who'd come to pass judgment on the care she provided the patient. She showed her into the study. Ramón was watching TV with his teenage son and daughter, who could hardly summon the effort to greet her politely. They displayed an apathy typical of nihilist philosophers or provincial museum guards.

Ramón signaled to his children to leave him alone with Teresa. He had written some lines in his notebook and passed them to her to read: *Thank you so much for coming. As my wife explained on the phone, there's nothing more to be done. I asked you for some of that stuff because last time it really helped, especially with walking—I'm having a hard time with that. The medications they've given me ease the pain itself, but don't take away the discomfort, if that makes any sense. Anyway, I wanted to thank you in person for all your help. It's been a pleasure getting to know you.*

Teresa answered that he wasn't going to get rid of her so easily. Ramón was flattered and smiled at the joke.

"Let's see how you like these cookies. They'll last you about two weeks, then I'll bring you some more. How does that sound?"

The look in Ramón's eyes asked her to be realistic. Teresa claimed that the cookies might have surprising results, then changed the subject.

"Will you introduce me to your parrot?"

Ramón rose from his seat with difficulty, and they went out into the garden. Teresa couldn't help but laugh at Benito's vulgar catcalls. She recalled aloud that her grandmother had had a parrot just like this one. It was her grandmother, she added, who'd taught Teresa to bake. At this stage in their relationship, she no longer needed to present an inscrutable façade to her patient. Thanatology wasn't a psychoanalytic process but a kind of grief counseling, a professional comfort service that could withstand a certain degree of familiarity.

They went back into the study. There, she asked Ramón to write about how he was coping emotionally with the pain. Ramón signaled that he didn't know what she meant. She asked if he sought comfort from his family or confided in them, if he ever allowed himself to be pampered.

All this is hard enough for them as it is. I'm resigned to my fate. This is no way to live. It'll be a relief for them when I'm gone.

"No, Ramón," she said gravely, "they're going to miss you. It'll be a huge loss for them. And you know what's going to help them move on? Feeling like they had some moments of connection with you and that you really knew each other. I know you might feel like a burden to them and that it would be best if . . . well. But there's something really important you still need to do for them. Say goodbye slowly, teach them how to say goodbye. Nobody tells you this, but it's something that can be learned. My grandmother taught us how. She sent for the priest and made sure he was offered his favorite sweets. She gave us all a gift and told us all something special. It was a master class in farewells. You've told me how strongly you feel about leaving your family an inheritance. Well, just like we teach children manners, this is something you need to teach them. You can't abandon your children just like that, otherwise how will they know what to do when their own time comes? . . . Think about it. And let me know how you like the cookies, okay?"

Their conversation was a game of chess on an infinite board. There were as many pawns as words, as many bishops as questions, as many knights as promises, as many rooks as insults. There was a king of great importance whose only available move was to hide from the final checkmate. It was a vast monosyllable, and each of its escapes was a no. There was a powerful, vulnerable queen risking her life with every move. No checkmate was more beautiful than hers. Yes.

24

The patches and cookies quieted the urge to escape from the pain. Pumped full of painkillers and bewildered by Teresa's words, Ramón postponed the advance preparations for his death. Gradually, he lost control of his legs. He suffered from coughing fits that sounded like a bag of popcorn exploding in a microwave oven.

When he saw Carmela come into the house pushing an empty wheelchair, Ramón caught sight of his own mournful, transparent ghost. An outrageous apparition. I'm not going to sit down in that fucking thing, he thought, and indeed he didn't, since the person to seat him in it was Elodia's son. In exchange for a meager fee, Antonio had agreed to come by each morning to carry Señor Martínez from his bed to the bathroom, and from the bathroom to the ground floor, where he left him settled into the wheelchair. In the afternoon, he came back and repeated the same routine in reverse. Compared with the sacks of cement Antonio had lugged around on construction sites from a young age, Ramón was a light, ergonomic package. The ease with which the young man carried him back and forth aggravated Ramón's sense of his own nonexistence.

I've been thinking about it, he told Benito. There's no other surefire method. I've got to put a bullet in me. One of my clients shot himself, once. He was drowning in debt, his wife was screwing her tennis coach, and his daughter had died in a car crash. He locked himself in his office and blew his brains out. I'll write Carmela a note: *Take me to my office, I want to sit at my desk.* I'm not going to kill myself here. They'd only wind up hating the house and having to move. I'll say I need to pick up some papers and take my briefcase to hide the gun in. I'll ask them to leave me alone in my office and sit at my desk, facing my framed photos and my law school diploma. I want Leonardo to be there when they find me. And I want them to hear the shot, so it won't be too traumatic. That's important. If they picture it before they see me, it won't be such a shock. And I'll put something over my head, a pillowcase or a sweater, so they won't see how I ended up. The tricky thing is getting to the key to open the drawer with the gun. We hid it in the closet, up on a shelf, and now I can't stand on a stool to reach it. According to the fucking law, assisting a suicide is punishable by two to five years of jail time. And that's just if it's indirect. If there's willful cooperation, if someone injects you with something or gives you the bullet, the sentence is harsher. But why the fuck should the state care, if you give your consent in writing for someone to help you?

Once again, Elodia was conscripted. One morning, Ramón asked to be left in the bedroom because he didn't feel like going downstairs. Once his wife and children had left, he rang the bell.

"What can I do for you?" Elodia asked, panting from the exertion of running upstairs.

Ramón had written out his instructions ahead of time.

Please take me to the dressing room. Climb onto that little stool and pass me the key on top of the closet. Over to the right, on the edge. Don't mention this to Mrs. Martínez, you saw how she freaked out about the watch.

"Don't tell me you're planning to sell something else in secret."

Ramón glowered at her. She obeyed. She climbed onto the stool and began feeling around for the key with her hand. He heard a light clink, the muted tap of metal on wood. There it is, thought Ramón, but Elodia kept groping around on the shelf.

"It's not there," Elodia said. She was congenitally inept at lying.

I just heard it, Ramón growled in his thoughts. Elodia turned around and was met with the sight of a lunatic gesturing frenetically for her to keep looking.

"Look at my hand, it's covered in dust," she said, playing dumb. "I'll come back and clean in a while. I'm sure it'll show up then."

Ramón insisted. You're not coming down from there until you hand me that key. I just heard it, you goddamned liar. Get it down. I know it's up there. I just heard it right now.

"What do you want it for?" Elodia asked.

Don't you get fresh with me, dammit. What do you care? Keep looking. Turn around and look.

"Calm down, we'll find it any minute," said Elodia as she began to search with exaggerated diligence. "Nothing but dust. Couldn't Señora Martínez have moved it?"

Ramón shook his head and pointed to his ear to let her know that he'd heard the key.

"Do you want me to call her cell phone?"

No, you fucking idiot, she can't find out about this. I heard it right there. Don't bother trying to fool me.

"You know what? Those beans are going to get burned. Let me go downstairs and turn down the stove."

No fucking way. You're not leaving here until you give it to me, you two-faced bitch. Carmela must've told you something. Keep looking. We'll see who blinks first.

"It must have fallen. I'm telling you it's not up there."

Liar. Do I have to spell it out for you? I'm getting my notebook. You will not betray me. Ramón lifted the brake on his chair and began to wheel himself backward. Elodia hurried down from the stool.

"Where do you want me to take you?"

I need my notebook.

She pushed him over to the chest where he'd left his notebook and pens.

"I'm just going to run down and turn off the beans," said Elodia while Ramón was writing. "Be right back."

Ramón grabbed her by the wrist. Don't you dare go anywhere.

"Please don't be angry."

Don't lie to me. What did my wife tell you?

"About what?" said Elodia, so nervous from lying that she was sweating profusely.

The key is up there. I heard it just now.

"It must've been something else. I moved one of Señora Martínez's purses."

Swear to God you didn't find it.

"It's a sin to take the Lord's name in vain. I'll keep looking right away but let me go turn off the beans. Pretty please. They're going to get burned."

Ramón didn't budge.

Think of what I've done for you and your family. You're betraying me. I beg you not to betray me now. Look at the shape I'm in.

"How could I not remember? I'm so grateful to you, it's just that . . ." She was on the verge of tears. "It isn't there, Señor Martínez, it isn't there."

She must've been sniffing around in the drawer. She's not stupid, she must know something.

Ramón changed strategies. He clasped his hands together as if in prayer. He showed his vulnerable side.

Elodia started to cry. She wiped her tears on her apron.

Ramón pointed at the closet again, plaintively.

"All right, let's see," said Elodia, apparently defeated.

She climbed back onto the stool and swept her hand over the shelf, her eyes brimming with tears and her lips bathed in snot. She paused where the key had clinked earlier. Ramón knew it was there. At that very moment, Elodia's fingers were touching the piece of metal, the only thing he needed to get hold of the gun and put himself out of his misery. Hurry up, he wailed silently, just grab it.

Elodia drew back her empty hand, lowered her arm, and stepped down from the stool. She was crying and trembling with shame. She couldn't bring herself to look at him.

"It's not there . . . I swear it's not there."

25

Paulina was seized by a mortal panic whenever she found her father sleeping with his head twisted into an odd position. Since he was connected to an artificial respirator day and night, it was impossible to tell if he was alive by checking his breath. She had to scrutinize other, more subtle signs: the trembling of his eyelids as he dreamed, the reddish color of his fingernails, the pulsing of a vein against the skin on his neck or wrist. In this way, she learned to examine her father in such painstaking detail that every so often when she was bored in class, she amused herself by sketching parts of his face and hands.

One Sunday morning when Carmela was out, Paulina went into the bedroom to check on her father and found him asleep with an open cookie tin on his lap. She tiptoed toward him. She was about to check his vital signs as she usually did, but the cookies caught her eye and whetted her appetite. Slowly, she reached a thieving hand into the tin.

The chocolate cookie had an aftertaste of oregano. It

must have been a wholesome, organic recipe. Despite its unusual flavor, Paulina ate another. It didn't taste as bad as the first. She felt a pleasant tickle on her tongue like a kind of fizzing, as if she'd taken a sip of ice-cold soda.

Twenty minutes later, she started feeling dizzy. She assumed it was a divine punishment for filching the cookies. She began to feel a stabbing, slow-motion sense of guilt, and considered purging her sins by making herself throw up. She thought of looking for Mateo so she would feel less alone in her angst, but lately he was so withdrawn and glued to his electronic appendages that Paulina scarcely recognized the zombie he had become. She had complained to her mother several times. She asked her to tell Mateo to be more attentive to their father, but Carmela only made excuses for him, appealing to the emotional incompetence of men.

Delirious from the effects of the cannabis, she went into the bathroom and splashed some water onto her face. In the mirror, she noticed her eyes were irritated and gleaming. She lost herself gazing into her pupils, her imperfect hazel irises, and the red blood vessels in the whites of her eyes. Never had she studied that hair-raising organ so closely. Then she was shocked by the completely inexplicable fact that she had two eyes but only one nose.

Staring at her nose, she began to crack up. Why was it so hilarious? She couldn't remember. Maybe the cookies were stale, rancid. I'm hallucinating. She went back to her bedroom and locked herself in. When she threw herself down, the springs in her bed squeaked like scampering rats. The idea of rats scurrying across the room amused her, and she laughed hysterically, rocking her pelvis back and forth to trigger the noise. Carried away by the rhythm, she gave herself over to a lascivious swaying that in the end looked like a demonic convulsion. Exhausted, she suddenly paused and laughed again. She'd never had so much fun. What was going on? What was she thinking? She couldn't remember, but she was feeling great.

26

"Have you been to the Cineteca lately?" Eduardo asked as soon as he'd stretched out on the couch.

The question, so frivolous and unexpected, distracted Teresa from her grief for her friend Lourdes, whom she'd met in the chemotherapy suite, and who, after years of remission, had suffered a relapse six months earlier. No one was safe from recurrence, no matter how many blueberries, limes, or pomegranates they consumed.

But something seemed to be going on with Eduardo. The simple fact of asking his analyst a personal question marked a tipping point in the transference process. She needed to take advantage of it.

"I used to go all the time," she said. "I love the movies."

Eduardo sat up on the couch and turned toward Teresa.

"Do you think it would be a clean enough place for me to go?"

The goal was to achieve a psychological shift. Stodgy moralists insisted that people could never change. Teresa accepted that everyone had an immutable core, a kind of soul in the secular sense—a piece of hardware, like the aluminum soul of a polyethylene pipe—but she believed that habits, ideas, and emotions could change. Eduardo's psychological soul stood alone, beyond the id, ego, and superego, the holy trinity of Freudian psychoanalysis. Freud himself had shown the way: where id was, there ego shall be. Beneath the disputed territories of these agencies of the personality lay the solid foundation of life, beyond the vagaries of circumstance, impervious to mutation. No matter what traumas, love affairs, or books changed a person's behavior, the soul continued to exist. Psychoanalysis was simply the search for that inescapable truth. Like the tragic heroes who'd served as inspiration for Freud, at some point everyone must come face-to-face with himself, experience recognition, achieve anagnorisis. For this to be possible one had to believe in a mental essence, and Teresa could find no word less stale than soul to describe it.

"Are you thinking of going to the Cineteca?"

"I don't know," said Eduardo. "I haven't been to a movie theater since I had leukemia. Ten years or more. My mom used to take me on Fridays."

Eduardo almost never mentioned his mother except to criticize one of her unhygienic habits. This was indeed a crucial session.

"What do you want to see?"

"A Syrian movie Emilia posted about on Facebook. She said it was the most beautiful film she'd ever seen and she was dying to see it again. I sent her a direct message and said I was dying to see it, too. I'd never even heard of it. She messaged me back and said 'Let's go,' with three exclamation marks. I told her I'd be out of town this weekend, so we agreed to go next week. Just thinking about it . . . What if she expects me to kiss her there, in the seats, in that fusty air? How will I be able to breathe? What if she gets popcorn? If she eats it with her hands I'll be so grossed out. If I kiss her it'll be so disgusting, I know it. I can't."

"What is it you're so disgusted by?"

"I . . . I don't know. Not her. Myself."

The truth was there, echoing in those words, in which Eduardo had finally confronted a clear reflection of himself. Now he was speechless. Teresa waited in silence, thinking that this was precisely the cure: to look at ourselves in the mirror is necessary to change our appearance—in this case the self, the psychological self-image. That was why Freud drew so extensively from classical tragedy, from the recognition that unites the hero with his destiny. Teresa remembered her own moment, not on a couch but in bed with her lover in a hotel room, when she told herself that she didn't want to be good. That same night she demanded a divorce from her husband. A twinge in her chest took her back to the depression that followed, the social opprobrium, her cancer, and her foolish self-reproach. The tumor was her own fault; according to the teachings of Wilhelm Reich, it was the suppuration of her soul. How she had hated herself when she read that charlatan's work. How disgusted she had felt, just like Eduardo.

"Why do you disgust yourself?"

"No, I mean because of everything I could pick up at the Cineteca. It's got to be dirtier than a regular movie theater. I read a study about English hospitals. They found out that there's thirty percent more bacteria per square foot in public hospitals than in private ones, although the bacteria in the private ones is more resistant to antibiotics. Obviously. But the point is, the cleaning leaves a lot to be desired. I checked to see if the film was showing at another theater, but it's not. It's not even available online. It was the last one to be filmed in Syria. They were already at war, it's not exactly romantic. It's about a little blind girl who recites the Koran. I guess Koran reciters are the rock stars of Islam. And the little girl has such a beautiful voice that rumor has it that Allah is bewitched by her and protects her from the bombs so they won't interrupt her recitals. And people believe it, so they gather around in massive groups during the bombings to hear her sing. But then some terrorists kidnap her and do horrible things to her and force her to sing for them in the barracks, all covered in blood. That part was in the trailer. It would be weird to kiss during a movie like that, right? Anyway, I don't know. Maybe she doesn't like me and she only said yes because she wants to see it again. And I'm going to come out of there covered in dust mites from God knows where. They'll eat me alive. If I could just disinfect the seat before she gets to the theater. But we'll probably meet up outside, right? They'd have to let me in half an hour early. But there'll be another movie showing then."

The decisive moment had passed, and Teresa had failed to seize it. She would have had to interrupt Eduardo before he took refuge in his phobia. Why hadn't she intervened in time? How had she been so distracted? Like the man with whom she'd thought she was happy, Eduardo was a rational automaton whose engine ran on the blood of a fearful child, the stifled child he carried inside him. The time had come to stray from her method.

"What's the movie called?" she asked.

"*By Night I Vanquished the Moon*. I know it sounds cheesy, but it won an important award at Cannes."

"It sounds good."

"I can't go. It'd be such a nightmare if I had an attack in front of Emilia. I'd have to take a mask in case I started feeling bad." Eduardo was talking about the panic attacks that his therapy with Teresa had helped him get under control. "And then what? I'd have to lie and say I have asthma, and it's not like that's too attractive, either. And apart from that, last night I read an article about a rabid raccoon that got into a movie theater in Dallas and bit three guys in the audience. One of them was unvaccinated because he was a Mormon or something. Two months later, he dropped dead. I started watching videos of rabid animals and people foaming at the mouth and hallucinating, terrified of water even though they were dying of thirst. Then suddenly it was five in the morning. Apparently, the strain of the virus carried by rodents is resistant to vaccination. What's the deal with viruses? They're not even alive and they can kill you. I don't know how people can live in a world like this."

"Why don't you visit the Cineteca ahead of time and see how you feel?"

"I can't take the risk."

"Of what? Getting bitten by a raccoon?" Teresa said, convinced that the time had come to sabotage the transference with dynamite.

Eduardo stared at her as if the rabies virus were already having an effect on his brain.

"My mother pays you to understand me, not to make fun of me just like she does."

"I'm trying to understand you."

Eduardo rose and began to fold up the sheet he used to cover the couch. Teresa felt like adding, in a sadistic outburst, "Don't you realize you're afraid of germs because you disgust yourself? You're disgusted by the photos of your bald head as a child, your deathly pale face, your mother in a surgical mask and gloves. You're disgusted by your penis and the wet dreams you can't control. You don't want her to castrate you or hollow you out like your mother. Do you know what that rabid raccoon is really called? Go ask Emilia. It's between her legs."

"Thanks," he said sarcastically, ready to leave.

"I'll go to the Cineteca with you. I'd love to see that movie."

Eduardo looked at her with the same bewilderment he reserved for his mother when she came home tipsy on a Friday evening.

"My treat," Teresa added.

Finally, Teresa was experiencing, without the fog of marijuana, one of those unlikely moments that saved her life from absurdity.

They bought tickets for the five o'clock screening and hung around for a while outside the theater. Dozens of moviegoers went by with enormous sodas and cartons of popcorn. Eduardo checked his watch constantly. An usher came over to ask if they were going to go in to the movie. Teresa told him they were thinking about it. They thought about it for another half hour. In the distance, they heard rapturous singing. They left as it began to get dark.

27

Ernesto had bribed the authorities, that fucking faggot. You betrayed your own brother, you're after my house, you predatory piece of shit. Ramón spat on him with glee the last time he came by to make threats. The doctor had signed his eviction order. Doctors and judges, the same kind of scum. Because Ernesto was footing the bill for Dr. Aldama's house calls. Your brother's helping us out, we can't afford it, Carmela had said. But it's an investment, that snake, so he can get hold of our assets. Ramón was going to assert his constitutional rights by filing a writ of protection based on Article 4, Paragraph 7 of the Constitution, the right to housing. You had it coming to you, asshole. It's a wild world out there without legal protection. I'm not paying up. Aldama's sentence is invalid. That debt was canceled when we were born to the same woman. You're not getting me out of here. I have ten business days to start the proceedings. What time is it? Ramón searched for his watch among the packets of pills. It wasn't where it should have been. Ernesto stole it. Carmela!

Where's my watch? I have to get to court. The ruling should take just long enough. Maybe a year. Where did I put my watch? Tell them I'm running late. I got held up, but I'm on my way. I was feeling a bit under the weather. Who are you? Let go of me, you piece of shit. Get your hands off me. Get your hands off me. How much did he pay you? Fucking police. Where's your arrest warrant? Put me down, you moron. Call Carmela. Tell her to file the writ of protection.

"Calm down," said Elodia. "It's just my son Toño."

Show me the arrest warrant. Let me go and I'll pay up. I have cash. How much do you want?

Ramón's bed had been set up in the study. Toño sat him in the wheelchair and pushed him out into the garden.

"Say hello to Benito," said Elodia. "Good morning, Benito. Señor Martínez is here to see you."

Get this fucking thing off me. I have the right to speak.

"That's your oxygen. Leave it where it is. Leave it there."

"Do you want me to strap him in?" asked Antonio.

"He'll calm down in a minute. I don't want him all bundled up like a tamale."

I don't want any tamales. Bring me a red *pozole* with some nice lean pork. What would you like? No really, it's on me.

"Cocksucker!"

"Look, he's already forgotten," Elodia said to her son. "Now get off to work."

They left Ramón dozing in the garden. He pulled off his oxygen mask in his sleep. Benito woke him.

"Son of a bitch!"

Carmela? Help me.

Benito was getting worked up.

"Son of a bitch! Son of a bitch!"

Elodia came outside to see what was going on.

"What is it now, Benito? What's the matter with . . ."

Ramón was convulsing. She knew that, when he had one of these fits, she was supposed to bring the inhaler and administer three puffs, to let him breathe. The oxygen mask had been tossed onto the grass. Ramón's lungs were filling with fluid, which the doctors extracted with an enormous needle. Elodia needed to rush upstairs for the medicine. If she didn't, Señor Martínez would suffocate. She knelt down at his side and held his agitated hands in hers.

"Son of a bitch! Son of a bitch! Son of a bitch!" the parrot screeched.

Each night, Elodia lit a candle and prayed for Ramón's eternal rest.

"Light my way, O Lord . . ."

Ramón opened his eyes, roused by a rush of adrenaline. Help.

"Our Father, who art in heaven . . ."

A flood of light, voices, Benito reciting Our Father, Elodia squawking, "Son of a bitch!" Carmela tasting a chorizo *sope*.

"Thy will be done, on earth as it is in heaven . . ."

Ramón's heart pounded like a drum, echoing through his consciousness. His system was rocked by a turbulent wave of endorphins.

"Forgive me, O Lord."

Elodia clung to Ramón's hands to help her withstand the harsh gaze of God. Just how serious was the sin she was committing? She was afraid. She desperately needed to pee. She tensed her abdominal muscles. She knew that when it was all over, before she dialed the thirteen digits of Señora Martínez's cell phone, she would make a stop in the bathroom. She would sit on the toilet and rehearse the lines as she relieved herself. Señora Martínez, it's Elodia. Benito would be the only one to witness the truth.

"Son of a bitch!"

She would tell Carmela that when she heard Benito squawking, she came out into the garden and found Señor Martínez asleep and at peace. She would take a sip of water before dialing Señora Martínez's number. Then she would deliver the news, and cry, and lie, and sin.

Elodia murmured a hodgepodge of prayers, while Benito paid jubilant tribute to Ramón's life.

"Lamb of God . . ."

"Son of a bitch!"

". . . You take away the sins of the world . . ."

"Son of a bitch!"

". . . only say the word and my soul shall be healed . . ."

"What the fuck? Son of a bitch!"

Ramón opened his mouth like a hungry chick seeking its mother.

A NOTE ABOUT THE AUTHOR

Jorge Comensal was born in Mexico City in 1987. He has received grants from the Fundación para las Letras Mexicanas and the Fondo Nacional para la Cultura y las Artes. His work has appeared in *Letras Libres*, *Este País*, *Nexos*, *Revista de la Universidad de México*, *VICE*, and *The Literary Review*, and his essay *Yonquis de las letras* was published in Spain in 2017. *The Mutations* is his first novel.

A NOTE ABOUT THE TRANSLATOR

Charlotte Whittle is a writer and translator. Her work has appeared in *The Literary Review*, *Guernica*, *BOMB*, the *Los Angeles Times*, and elsewhere. Her translation of Norah Lange's *People in the Room* was published in 2018. She lives in New York and is an editor at Cardboard House Press.